秘 HIDDEN

Coming Soon

Warned
A Mei-hua Adventure

Trapped
A Mei-hua Adventure

To discover more stories
about Mei-hua and Ancient China visit
http://padevoe.com/?page_id=177.

HIDDEN

A Mei-hua Adventure

P.A. De Voe

Drum
Tower
Press
St. Louis, Missouri

First Edition. First Printing, 2015

Printed in the United States of America

Publisher's Note
This is a work of fiction. Names, characters, places, and incidents either are the product of the author's imagination or are used fictitiously, and any resemblance to actual persons, living or dead, business establishments, events, or locales is entirely coincidental.

Cover design by Kelly Cochran

Library of Congress Control Number: 2014921965

Published by
Drum Tower Press, LLC
165 Bon Chateau Drive
Saint Louis, Missouri 63141-6081
http://padevoe.com/?page_id=177

ISBN-10: 1942667000
ISBN-13: 978-1-942667-00-1

DEDICATION

To my daughter Renée, who inspired me,

and

to Ron, who encouraged me

ACKNOWLEDGEMENTS

This book has been a long time in the making and I would like to thank my many beta readers who encouraged me in this endeavor over the years. I would also like to thank Jennifer Hasheider, former president of our local Saturday Writer's group, who generously offered initial editorial guidance. And of course, I owe a debt of gratitude to Renée DeVoe Mertz, editor-in-chief for Drum Tower Press, for her excellent and conscientious, yet diplomatic, editing process.

Finally, I would like to thank my fellow Sisters in Crime writer, Kelly Cochran, for all her advice and help in producing *Hidden*.

Any errors in this novel are mine alone.

Who are the people in Mei-hua's world?

This story is set in 1380, the beginning of the Chinese Ming Dynasty.

Zhang Mei-hua	Our heroine
Zhang Xue-wen	Mei-hua's father
Old Lin	Mei-hua's family servant
Nanny	Mei-hua's nanny
Young Chen	Servant
Ben-ji	Kidnapper
Mother Yang	Ben-ji's mother
Da-shan	Ruffian
Ping-an	Mei-hua's mistress
Guei-lung	Ping-an's brother
Madam Wu	Ping-an's mother
Aunt Xi	Ping-an's aunt
Auntie Lao	Ping-an's elderly aunt
Orchid	Ping-an's senior maid
Lily	Ping-an's maid
Master Hsu Dou-wu	Ping-an's father
Uncle Fei	Ping-an's uncle
Gran'ma Fei	Madam Wu's brother-in-law's mother
Teacher Song	Ping-an's teacher
Mr. Mu	The carpenter
Mrs. Mu	The carpenter's wife

CHAPTER 1

"MEI-HUA! WAKE UP! Now! You don't have much time to dress. You must get up! "

Stirring, Mei-hua pulled a soft, silken quilt over her until only a few ruffled black strands of hair peeked out from under it.

"Mei-hua! There is no time! You must go!"

Cool air struck her face as the quilt came away. Sleepy and irritated, she squinted into the light. A wrinkled, worried face outlined by steel gray hair pulled straight back into a bun, hovered over her. Mei-hua closed her eyes while raising an arm and blocking the piercing light. After a moment, however, she moaned in protest while pushing the quilt further away and looked around. A comfortable, colorful room greeted her.

Three white, cylindrical paper lanterns hung from the ceiling's open beams, filling the room with a warm glow. Long, slender sheets of paper covered the walls. Some had watercolor paintings of insects perched on plants; others displayed Chinese characters written with powerful, black brush strokes—short poems about the Mei-hua flower, a symbol of strength and loyalty. Her father had the poems changed regularly to encourage her good behavior. A large bundle of fresh cut branches filled with small white flowers sat on a highly polished, wooden table nearby. Shaking her head in not-quite-awake confusion, she threw aside the cover and stumbled out of bed.

Without giving Mei-hua time to collect her thoughts, the elderly woman helped her change into a luxurious pair of loose, dark pants, a high-collared blouse, and a supple, knee-length cotton jacket.

Mei-hua stood quietly, still sleepy, unconsciously stroking her clothing. This was her favorite outfit. Somehow its softness and simple geometric pattern of sapphire over midnight blue reminded her of her mother, a woman she never knew.

"Hurry, Mei-hua! You're taking too much time! Your father will not be pleased!"

She stepped closer to her nanny, who quickly tied Mei-hua's lustrous, jet black hair back at the nape of her neck and, with a final, critical inspection, pronounced her fit to leave the room.

"Now, go! Your father is waiting!"

"I..." Mei-hua stammered, still half-asleep, "Where is he? Where should I go?"

"To his study. He's been up all night." The woman shook her head. "Something happened; something is wrong." With a look of concern, she examined her young charge carefully. "Why are you so sleepy? Nothing happened here tonight, did it? No foxes, no ghosts?" she asked while casting a penetrating glance around the room.

Mei-hua grinned and shook her head. "No. No foxes or ghosts."

The older woman frowned. "Don't laugh. Everyone knows foxes are rascals, getting people to do all sorts of strange things. They've even been known to take human form and entice young children away from their families. Problems do not come by themselves; something has to bring them to us."

Still watching Mei-hua for anything unusual, in case a fox spirit had enchanted her charge, the nanny glumly added, "Never underestimate what they can do. I still remember the mischief one played on my family."

Mei-hua had heard the story before, many times.

"Yes, Nanny," she said. "When you were only three years old, a fox spirit lived in your house. It played tricks on you and your family, dropping dirt in a bowl of noodles and making your newly bought chicken's feathers change from white to brown."

The older woman nodded somberly. "That's right. We were only able to force it out of our home after we burned incense for many days and a Daoist priest did an exorcism. The exorcism was expensive but it had to be done."

Mei-hua glanced at the kindly face etched with concern, then away. Although Nanny was now elderly, the fox story from her childhood remained as clear as if it had happened yesterday. It seemed to be the most memorable event in her life and she often repeated the tale.

To reassure the well-meaning woman about the fox spirit, Mei-hua again said, "No, no foxes or ghosts. I was groggy, but I'm fine now."

"Yes, you were still too sleepy. Poor child." With a mournful gaze, she held Mei-hua's face between gnarled hands and patted her cheeks. "Even in sleep, you share your father's heart. Yes, something is wrong. I, too, can feel it. Go, see him; he will tell you whatever is necessary."

Mei-hua stepped out onto the veranda. All of the rooms on the first floor opened onto this porch, which served as the central artery for moving around the house. She briefly peered into the veranda's open center, barely visible now in the evening light. Unseen blooming flowers filled the night air with a spicy sweetness. While these fragrances floated around her, a sliver of light, escaping from behind dark clouds, peeped out at her and was dimly reflected in a small pond. This whisper of light brought unclear, looming shapes into view. She paused, staring into the blackened garden. The monoliths were massive craggy stones brought from the sacred mountain Tai Shan. Their presence soothed her.

Soundlessly, she moved around the veranda until she came to a closed door. A light squeezed out under it as if to create a welcome mat. With a gentle touch, she knocked and, without waiting, pushed open the door and entered. Her father sat in a circle of light at a heavy, deeply carved desk. Head bent over a sheet of rice paper, he concentrated on his writing; his brush moved quickly and surely across the paper's surface. At the click of the closing door, he looked up.

"My daughter." His voice held a world of sorrow. She stopped halfway across the room and stood silently observing the slender, elegant man. Indeed, Nanny was right, something was very wrong. She had never heard her father speak in such a tone before.

"Come here, my dearest," he said. Even though she was almost a young woman, her father continued to use many terms of endearment. For, as he often said, she would always be his child, no matter her age.

She stepped behind the desk and he put an arm around her shoulders.

"Mei-hua, tonight I am going to send you on an errand and I want you to be extremely careful, because you are going to take care of my most precious possession."

A surge of pride shot through her. Her father was the district's magistrate. Therefore, all of the government's responsibilities—both civil and criminal—were his responsibilities. In criminal cases, he was the judge, investigator, and prosecutor. Although he had staff and officers to help him, he worked long hours to ensure justice for the people of his district. Sometimes he appeared so tired she feared for his health.

Despite Mei-hua's young age, his work had always fascinated her. She was confident that, if he would let her, she could help him and then he would not be so exhausted. Now he wanted her help. This was her chance to prove herself.

"Yes, father. I'm ready to help you with whatever you need. I've studied hard. I can read, do arithmetic, and write with a good, steady hand. I'm ready to be of assistance."

Her father's eyes smiled at her declaration, though his lips did not.

"Thank you, Mei-hua. I can always count on you, but I don't need that kind of help. I have a competent, hard working staff and many good officers. No, that's not what I need."

At Mei-hua's disappointed frown, he added, "No, my dear, this is more important than office work."

Mei-hua held her breath and waited for his next

words. In the eyes of the world she was only a girl, but her father knew she was special. She again straightened her shoulders; she would help him, no matter what the cost.

Her father sighed. Then began, "Perhaps you noticed all the people coming and going, more than usual." He wiped a hand over his eyes. "In my work as District Magistrate, I've made enemies. Powerful enemies who speak directly into the Emperor's ear. Recently, a complicated case involving mismanagement of government monies has been of great concern to me." He looked into his daughter's eyes as if deciding whether to continue.

After a moment, he went on, "I am telling you this, because it's critical for you to fully understand the seriousness of our situation. I know you're intelligent and will keep everything I say hidden in your heart. Our lives depend on your doing the right thing."

Her head spun. This was even bigger than she'd expected. Her father didn't want her to do some little office task; he wanted her to share in a government problem. She grasped his hand to show her willingness while, at the same time, hoping he didn't think she was showing too much pride. He always reminded her of the importance of being modest. She didn't want him to change his mind at confiding in her because she appeared too bold or impetuous.

Lowering his voice, he continued, "The details are not important; however, you must know that I have influential and unscrupulous enemies who are at this very moment trying to destroy the House of Zhang."

House of Zhang. Her father only used this phrase when he meant every member of his entire family, including her uncles, aunts, and cousins far and near.

Mei-hua listened to his every word as if her life depended on it. Because it did.

CHAPTER 2

"I DON'T WANT to frighten you, my little one, but to protect you I must be sure you understand the seriousness of this situation. As I've said, my enemies are corrupt and ruthless. To win, they are willing to do anything. Lie to the Emperor himself, tamper with documents; anything, everything to create the illusion of my working against the Emperor and the Ming Dynasty."

The government for the new dynasty had been established only eleven years before after many, many years of fighting. Mei-hua had heard terrible rumors about Emperor Ming Hong-wu's constant hunt for traitors, or anyone, no matter how insignificant, threatening his authority. His suppression of any signs of danger to his throne was quick and thorough. Whoever was trying to frame her father placed him in mortal danger. For the first time, a chill of fear overtook her.

"Over the past year," her father continued, "I've been working on a case involving large-scale tax fraud and a devious scheme to divert government monies into a private fund. This is one of the most serious types of treason because it undermines the Emperor's ability to establish and run a government acceptable to the people. If the people aren't on his side, they will revolt and his regime will end before it's begun.

"Last week I was able to find an informer. Unfortunately, even though he was an important link to the master-mind, he didn't know the leader's identity." He sighed, then added, "I'm close; I know it.

"Because I'm so close, the criminal has begun using extreme measures and distorting evidence to convince the Emperor I'm the treasonous party. I'm afraid if he's able to convince the Emperor of my guilt, we will all die. Everyone in our entire family."

There was no doubt what he said was true. Emperor Ming Hong-wu was infamous for his merciless treatment of those he thought threatened him in any way. Hundreds of people had already been executed under his rule because he suspected them—even without proof—of acts against him and his new government. Mei-hua shuddered with apprehension.

As if to reassure her, her father tried to smile, saying, "We're in trouble, my little bird, but we're also in the right. Our family will survive."

Mei-hua smiled in return, but her confidence faded as the icy fingers of fear reasserted their grip. If the Emperor believed they were criminals, and especially if he thought they were committing crimes against his rule, where would they be safe? She had always been taught the Emperor could see everywhere, even into the smallest corner of the Chinese Empire. He not only used all of the officials at his disposal to gather information, but also had a network of spies who kept him apprised of possible problems or challenges to his reign.

Maintaining an impassive face, her father hid his emotions. "Yes, we will survive. Nevertheless, we must be careful."

He shifted back into his chair and took up the rice paper covered with strong, clear characters. "This is a letter to a good friend of mine. In order to keep you safe, I'm going to send you to stay with him and his family. They'll claim you are a distant relation who has come to visit. You cannot stay with any of our own family, since we are all in danger until I solve this case.

"You'll leave for Hangzhou City tonight."

Hangzhou! A city famous for its beauty and culture. The name was almost magical to Mei-hua. She had heard so many things about it: the gardens, the stunning buildings, its size! She had wanted to visit Hangzhou for a long time. But, now that she was actually going there, she was miserable.

"No, Papa," she said, using a diminutive she hadn't spoken in years. "I won't leave. I'll remain here, at home, with you. What kind of daughter would I be if I ran away?"

"A dutiful daughter," her father replied, trying to hide an unbidden grin at her willful comments. "You want to be brave. You are brave. And you are also smart enough to realize our family is more secure if we disperse throughout the country. You must go." He shifted in his chair.

"The only problem I have left is exactly how I can get you safely to Hangzhou. Your nanny and Old Lin will travel with you, of course. I have not yet decided how large a contingent of guards would be best to send with you. Even though the revolution is over, bands of thieves still roam the countryside attacking defenseless travelers."

Mei-hua tried to interrupt, but her father continued.

"Go to my old friend. I've prepared everything. Even now your nanny is packing your things. You won't travel as a government official's daughter. I've decided it will be safer if you travel in disguise: you'll go as a common peasant until you reach Hangzhou. There, as far as everyone else is concerned, you'll be a poor relative of my friend. Old Lin will take all of the information and this letter of introduction. As I said, both Nanny and Old Lin will travel with you. I trust them because they've been with you since birth. Their loyalty is unquestionable."

"Papa, please let me stay! I belong here with you!"

"No, you must do as I say. By remaining in this house, you are more vulnerable each day. Listen to me, and don't be so stubborn!" His voice rose to a shout and he pushed forward in his chair, slamming his right hand on its broad wooden arm.

His shouting was like a slap to Mei-hua. A buzzing sensation ran around inside her head and she could barely breathe. Her father had never raised his voice to her before.

Reacting to her shock, her father reached out and gently patted her shoulder. He took a deep breath before continuing. "Mei-hua, I'm sorry, but you must realize how serious this situation is. For your sake, for my sake, you must go to Hangzhou. I could not bear to lose you as I..." He paused with a pained expression on his face.

She knew he was thinking of her mother. She had died within days of giving birth to Mei-hua. He had just taken his first position as magistrate in another distant province; none of his immediate family lived in the area, as was prescribed by the government for their magistrates. He had been away on business and blamed himself for her death, believing if he had been home he could have personally overseen her treatment and care. The only image Mei-hua had of her mother was a small, delicate painting. She sat in a high backed chair, wearing a vibrant blue gown. The stern expression the artist gave her could not dampen her beauty or the warmth in her eyes.

After his wife died, he transferred all of his love to Mei-hua, their only child. Although a busy and important man with many responsibilities, he and Mei-hua spent hours in each other's company, playing games, writing, or reading.

"I'm sorry, father; I'll do as you wish," she said, guilt washing through her for causing him more concern. Fortunately, however, the sharp sound of his hand on the desk jolted her enough to make her brain start working again, allowing her to break fear's debilitating grip.

She continued, with as much polite care as any good Chinese child would show when talking to her parent, "But may I make a suggestion? You said bandits are along the roads waiting to attack travelers and, at the same time, the government shouldn't be aware of my going to Hangzhou. If we travel with guards, we may be protected from the bandits, but most certainly the government will be able to detect where we are."

Her father nodded. Frowning, he passed a hand over his forehead.

"Yes, that's the dilemma. I'm still working on the details of your travel so as to avoid the government's attention."

"I have an idea. I am sure it will work!" she said, perking up.

He smiled. One thing his daughter did not lack was confidence.

"If my nanny, Old Lin, and I are to reach Hangzhou, we must travel alone."

He started to raise his hand in protest at this suggestion.

Her heart sank. If he didn't want to hear her idea, she couldn't argue with him. No father would accept such cheekiness.

He sighed. Then, instead of stopping her, he waved his hand for her to continue. "Go on."

Mei-hua spoke in a rush. "If we travel with armed guards, everyone, government officials and bandits, will know who we are. We'll appear out-of-place to the officials and wealthy to the bandits. Otherwise, why would we have guards?

"On the other hand, if we three travel as simple servants on our way to Hangzhou—the two older ones accompanying a young household servant for a wealthy family—no one will pay us any mind. We'll be too unimportant."

"My dear, you don't look like a household servant, and your speech will instantly give away your status as a daughter from an important house. Without guards, other people can get too close to you and notice things they might not otherwise notice. Eventually, someone will realize you cannot be a simple servant."

Mei-hua listened, her head tipped to one side. What he said was at least partially true. Of course, changing her appearance would be easy enough. All she needed was a simple change of clothing and a more casual hairstyle to blend in with the crowds on the street. The real problem was her speech: her language was Mandarin, the official language of China, and she spoke it the way only the educated, upper classes did. However, the majority of people in the area did not speak Mandarin as their first language, their home language. Therefore, if and when they did use Mandarin, they spoke with quite distinctive accents and rhythms.

Then she brightened, "Yes. That might happen if I spoke." She paused. "But what if I pretended to be mute? Then my voice, my accent, cannot give me away."

He stroked his chin, considering her ideas. After a long pause, he said, "It's possible. Dangerous, yes. But such a bold plan might work. At least it may have a better chance than traveling with armed soldiers."

Before she could say anything further, a servant rushed in with the message:

The Emperor's soldiers were at the gate!

CHAPTER 3

AT THIS NEWS, Mei-hua's father held her at arm's length. With his hands still on her shoulders, he cautioned her, "The worst has happened, my little one. The soldiers are here. You must leave with Nanny and Old Lin right away. They are your servants, but in many ways they have also been your teachers." He paused before smiling at his daughter and continuing. "And as we both know, you need as many teachers as we can find to tame you." He grinned again and then continued, "Listen to them. Follow their advice.

"I'm also sending young Chen Du along: he can do the heavy work, carry boxes, whatever Old Lin cannot do. Let's hope the four of you won't attract attention traveling as ordinary peasants."

Mei-hua threw her arms around him and buried her head into his neck, breathing in the musk of his clothing. What would she do without him? As long as she could remember it had always been the two of them, together. A small family, yes, but still a family.

He hugged her a moment before removing her arms and holding her back. With his hands resting heavily on her shoulders, he said, "You must go, my daughter, for both our sakes. Alone I can fight with all the legal means available to me, but with you here I'll always be vulnerable. You can, and will, be threatened. Through you, my enemies will get to me."

Mei-hua knew he was right. She told herself she had to be strong; that, in time, everything would return to normal. She stood straight and tall. "Father, I will do whatever you need."

"You are your mother's daughter," he said with a smile, though tears touched his eyes. Her father often told her how brave her mother was. She was born in western China and belonged to a different ethnic group, not Han like her father and most Chinese. She was Uyghur and came from a proud, well-educated family. In fact, both her mother's grandfather and father had worked with the previous Yuan dynasty's government, acting as go-betweens for the Mongol rulers and their subjects, the Han Chinese. This meant that during the revolution against the Yuan dynasty, they were in constant danger from those who eventually overthrew the old regime. This proved to be one reason her family allowed their daughter to marry a Han man; they believed it would keep her safe. No one paid attention to wives. Once a woman was married, she became virtually invisible. Being invisible was the same as being safe in Mei-hua's mother's case. Nevertheless, she remained proud of her ethnicity and heritage, and never hid the fact that she was Uyghur.

"My father's, too," Mei-hua returned, touching the writing brush and inkstone on his desk.

"Yes, and your father's, too." Then, as though giving her his everyday instructions, he added, "Be sure and study your characters. Continue your work on the Confucian classics. Put your best efforts into understanding them."

"Yes, Father," Mei-hua replied as she did every morning when he encouraged her to study hard. She pushed back a nearly overpowering urge to cry. Instead, she quoted a Confucian saying she knew he admired, "The Master said, 'Learning without thought is labor lost; thought without learning is perilous.'"

"You needn't show off your little knowledge; you've a lot more to learn," he chastised her, although he could not keep the gleam of amusement out of his eyes.

Old Lin, who had silently entered the room and was standing near the door, shuffled discretely to let his Master know time was running out.

"Never mind, Old Lin, we have a few minutes. I'm sure the soldiers are going to pretend they're here on other government business. They want to catch me unaware."

He removed the silken cord tied around his neck. A piece of jade half as long as Mei-hua's index finger hung from it. Gently, he slipped the cord over his daughter's head. "Keep this jade with you at all times. Don't let anyone else see it; wear it under your clothing."

He held the tea-colored oval toward the light, which illuminated dark characters engraved on its surface. Mei-hua read, "When the wind blows, the grass must bend."

Her father nodded; his gaze fell heavily upon his daughter. "War may have ended for our country, but our family is in greater danger than ever. This amulet speaks of the importance of wisdom and of doing what is right." He stroked the jade's glossy surface. "It's also a symbol of friendship and trust. Wear it and it will protect you. Follow its guidance until we are reunited."

He turned to his faithful servant. "Old Lin, take her back to Nanny. She should remove these clothes and put a simple peasant's cotton shirt and pants on Mei-hua. The four of you should leave for Hangzhou as soon as possible."

He reached into his wide sleeve and pulled out a package wrapped in paper and tied with a string. "Take this. The silver and gold in this package are more than enough to cover all of Mei-hua's expenses. More will come later." With that, he handed the package to Old Lin, adding, "Do you have all the official travel documents needed to pass from here to Hangzhou?"

The elderly servant was wearing a billowing, cotton peasant's jacket, tied at the waist. He touched its folds indicating where he carried the papers.

Mei-hua and her father embraced for the last time. She clenched her teeth as she held back the rivulet of tears threatening to run down her cheeks.

"Behave and be brave. Whatever you do should bring honor to the Zhang family name. Most importantly, remember we will be together again. This crisis will pass." He hugged her once more before he let her go.

Even though she wanted desperately to cry, she put on a brave face for her father. She would not let him down.

CHAPTER 4

THEY HURRIED down the veranda toward her room; however, when they reached her bedroom door, Old Lin did not stop. Instead, he led her to the kitchen located near the back garden gate. Mei-hua, as the daughter of the great house, had never seen this dim room before. Upon entering, all she could see was a brick stove running the length of the wall. The scent of ginger, garlic, onion, and other spices she couldn't identify filled the air. Breathing in the cooking fragrances, she was again almost overcome with a sense of impending loss. Would she come home again? What was going to happen to her, to her father? What lay ahead?

A movement to her left caught her eye and she turned. Nanny stepped out of the shadows, holding a limp, dark bundle.

"Old Lin, wait outside. She must change her clothes

now, before we go out of the compound," Nanny said.

Nodding, Old Lin soundlessly disappeared out the door.

Acting quickly, Nanny helped Mei-hua out of her brightly embroidered, fine cotton clothing and into the plain, coarse peasant outfit. While murmuring sympathetically, Nanny continuously reassured the young girl her separation from her father and her home would not be long.

Mei-hua wanted to believe her, but a weight pressed hard against her heart. Would she ever really be with her father again? The same questions kept filling her mind. She shivered in the warm room.

"Ah! You're cold! Here, I have a quilted jacket for you." At that, Nanny pulled out a rather dingy looking coat.

Mei-hua had seen this same type of outer layer in the streets of the city many times. But, as she stared at it now, she couldn't help thinking she had never truly been aware of how thin and ugly it was! Did this thing really provide even a little warmth? It seemed too flimsy, too light.

Guessing her reaction, Nanny commented as she helped Mei-hua into the jacket, "I know it isn't much, but it will provide the camouflage you need to get to safety. This is what most of the farmers wear."

Embarrassed that her feelings were so easily read, and sorry about her snobbish attitude, Mei-hua pulled the worn, quilted piece over her chest.

"This coat is just right. It's exactly what I need," she said as she tied it into place.

Once they left the kitchen, Mei-hua noticed Chen Du had joined Old Lin outside on the veranda. Chen Du, although not yet a man, stood tall and broad shouldered next to the slightly bent elder servant.

Upon seeing the two emerge from the doorway, Old Lin left the veranda and seemed to melt into the back garden. Nanny flapped her hand downwards, indicating Mei-hua should walk behind her. Chen Du followed the trio, keeping an eye on the inner chambers, watching for soldiers. They walked past dark rows of newly planted vegetables and herbs which, once mature, the cook would use to flavor many delicious dishes. Mei-hua wondered how long it would be before she would eat at home again.

Finally, they exited from the garden through a small door in the large stone wall which encircled their sprawling house and grounds. The small back street outside their compound was almost empty. The air was sharp and fresh. At this late hour most people were home asleep. No one would notice the odd four-some moving rapidly through the maze of lanes.

This was the first time Mei-hua actually walked in a public place. Whenever she went out of the house, her father's servants carried her in a wooden palanquin on their shoulders. The carriage's dark curtains allowed her to peek out at the street scenes without anyone being able to see her. It was not proper to walk openly in the streets among strangers. In spite of her apprehension about leaving her home and her father, Mei-hua felt a surge of excitement at this unexpected adventure.

She caught a whiff of incense when they passed the neighborhood's old, brilliantly painted temple. Its upturned eaves formed a black silhouette against the moon-filled night sky. After walking down one street and up another for what seemed forever, they eventually arrived at a small, though respectable, house near the city gate. This turned out to be Old Lin's nephew's home.

A middle aged man with a pleasant, square face met them at the door. After exchanging a few comments with his uncle in lowered voices, the man bowed to Mei-hua and led her and Nanny to an inner room. A kang, a low platform, filled most of the room. She could make out the forms of a couple of silent figures lying on it, asleep. The nephew's wife and daughter lay breathing softly, unaware of their presence. Nanny laid out two bed rolls, one for Mei-hua and one for herself. Stretching out on the solid and unfamiliar kang, Mei-hua, more tired than she realized, fell asleep as soon as her head touched the bed roll.

CHAPTER 5

TOO SOON, the window filled with morning light and Nanny gently nudged Mei-hua awake. Still thinking she was dreaming, she opened her eyes and saw two strange women sleeping in her bed. No, wait, not her bed. She was in their bed.

Then she remembered everything that happened during the previous night and once again had to force down the rush of panic. One thought stood out in her mind: she must reach Hangzhou.

Quickly and quietly, without disturbing Old Lin's nephew's wife and daughter, Mei-hua got down from the kang while Nanny rolled up their bedding. Without waiting for breakfast, the four headed for the city gates. Each night the gates were closed, and under no circumstances was anyone allowed to enter or leave the city. Each morning the gates were thrown open and farmers, merchants, and travelers went in and out freely. Mei-hua's little troupe, however, could not be so confident about their exiting the city. It was possible the solders had closed off the gate, looking for Mei-hua, the magistrate's daughter.

Once near the gates, they merged with a jostling crowd leaving the city. A contingent of soldiers stood just inside the enormous doors, overseeing the groups of people passing by, making sure all was orderly and safe. Taking a bundle of clothing from Nanny, Mei-hua mimicked the walk of the peasant girl in front of her. At the same time, the other three also kept their heads down and walked with the longer peasant gait. Their escape plan worked: the soldiers no more than glanced at them as they filed through the gates along with the other travelers.

Safely outside the city walls, they allowed themselves to smile and exchange a few words of encouragement. But there was no time for self-congratulations; they had a long road ahead of them from their home in Changsha City, Hunan Province. They had to travel by land for many days before eventually arriving in Hangzhou City on China's sea coast.

As they walked along the dusty road cutting through the valley outside Changsha City, Mei-hua looked at the fertile farming country and wondered when she would see its lush fields again. She thought of the lake north of the city, the shimmering Ding Ting Hu where she went every summer. Would she ever get to spend another long summer on its banks? Her thoughts bounced back and forth between sadness at leaving and excitement at being on the road. And underneath all her thoughts, pushed down to the bottom of her mind, remained the terror that the Emperor would destroy them all.

They had walked for a couple of hours when they passed a temple complex, its green roof tiles gleaming in the bright morning sun. In front of the commanding entrance gate a tiny woman sat selling rice cakes. Old Lin stopped and bought enough for all of them, along with a bowl of pork swimming in its own grease. The plain food was more than welcome to Mei-hua, who had developed quite an appetite.

While they ate, Old Lin wandered past the temple and stood talking to a farmer hauling farm produce to Changsha City. Trying not to appear curious, Mei-hua watched the two, wondering at the lively conversation. The farmer waved his arm toward his cart and then down the road. Old Lin nodded, answered at length, and removed a small package from his jacket. He opened it and dropped something into the farmer's hand. The farmer smiled and bowed slightly as if thanking him.

Soon Old Lin walked back to the little food stall where Mei-hua, Chen Du, and Nanny sat hunched down on their heels, just as the other people eating around them did. Old Lin spoke in a quiet voice to Chen Du, who went off in the direction of the cart.

Finally, the old servant took a handful of rice cakes and then dropped onto his heels, squatting on the ground next to Mei-hua. In a low voice he told her he had purchased the cart and oxen for their trip. Mei-hua glanced over at the rough, wooden cart with its immense, wooden wheels and nodded. It did not look at all comfortable, not at all like her carved, lacquered palanquin with silk curtains. Yet, she was happy with their new purchase; their ruse of being traveling peasants became more believable all the time.

———

While relishing the new sights and sounds of their journey, of the different kinds of people and places they were seeing, she admitted only to herself how unexciting travel itself was. She had heard so much about other people's trips, she had been sure every minute must be memorable. However, each day was much like the other: uneventful and uncomfortable. The cart bounced and jilted too much for Mei-hua to tolerate riding in it for long. Nanny, clutching the jarring wagon's side, usually sat perched on the front seat next to Chen Du, who drove the oxen. Mei-hua often walked along beside or ahead of the cart, accompanying Old Lin.

While pretending to be mute, Mei-hua delighted in taking on more and more of the mannerisms of the peasants they met daily, and she listened closely to the rhythm and pattern of their speech. When no one else was around, she liked to entertain Old Lin with her impersonations of the local peasants. If nothing else, it helped to pass the time as they walked for hours each day.

After what seemed like endless days of traveling, they were on the last leg of their journey to Hangzhou City. Unfortunately, travelers along the road reported bandit activity up ahead. Rather than be exposed to this new danger on land, they decided it would now be safer to travel by boat. They planned to sell their cart and oxen at the next village along the Jiang River. In the meantime, with the growing darkness, Old Lin announced they would stop at the first house they came to and ask for shelter.

"Can't we continue through to the village, Old Lin?" Mei-hua pleaded. She hated to admit it, but the journey exhausted her. When she rode in the cart, the unyielding, wooden bench made her seat hurt, and when she walked next to the cart for miles at a time, her legs cramped from the unusual exercise. "There might be a hostel where we could get rooms. It would be so good to be in a decent bed tonight instead of sleeping on someone's floor."

Old Lin nodded. "Yes, sleeping in a good bed is tempting, but don't forget the warnings about the possibility of bandits. They are often thick as ghosts at night. And already the road is deserted. Most people have found shelter for the night. It would be foolish to take a chance now that we have come so far."

Mei-hua pouted slightly. "I don't see any place to stay anyhow. Are we going to have to go back to the village we passed two miles ago?"

"No, of course not." With a glance at the sun hanging low in the sky, Old Lin sighed. "Okay, we'll go on. There will probably be another village or temple within the next couple of miles. We can stay at whatever we find next." Squinting, he strained to see down the road. "I just hope we find a place before the sun goes down in the next hour or so."

Mei-hua was about to reply when a group of men caught her eye. They were moving quickly across the fields, coming towards them.

"Maybe they can tell us about a good place to stay the night. That is, if you don't want to continue on to a nice, soft, warm bed," she added mischievously. As she spoke, her father's amulet grew hot against her chest. Without thinking about it, she shifted her shoulders to move the amulet away from her skin.

Mei-hua and Old Lin stood on the road watching the men as they came closer. Chen Du spoke first, "They don't look like farmers. Not merchants, either."

She realized he was right. The approaching men carried no hoes or tools, as farmers would, and they wore boots that would be ruined in the rice paddies. If they were merchants, they should have had boxes or loads to sell, but they carried no extra weight. At the same time, she became aware of how vulnerable they were, trapped on the open road. There was no shelter, no protection they could use to defend themselves if these men were dangerous. Their only option was to wait for the strangers to approach and hope they appeared too penniless to be worth robbing. She glanced at Nanny sitting stiff and silent on the cart. Watching.

Mei-hua caught Old Lin's attention. Without a word passing between them, they agreed to continue the ruse of being simple peasants. It allowed them to escape Changsha City, maybe now it would help them get safely through the rest of the trip to Hangzhou City.

Inexplicably, the jade amulet continued to radiate heat against her skin and she thought she heard a quiet voice say, "To be successful in war, deceive."

She quickly glanced around. Where did the voice come from? Was the amulet warning her?

Now the group of six rough-looking men strutted arrogantly down the center of the road making it impossible for anyone, much less the cart, to pass by them. As they approached, they stopped talking to each other and silently walked toward Mei-hua's group. Their silence made her more nervous than if they had been loud and boisterous.

The strangers halted in front of them, forming a human wall blocking their way. The jade amulet burned under her jacket. One word, *deceive*, echoed over and over again in her mind.

A man with skin the color of the dirt beneath his feet and a long, red scar on his neck swaggered up to Old Lin, stopping just short of plowing over the elder. Mei-hua, who had been walking down the road next to him, remained silent, fighting against the knot growing in her stomach.

"Who are you and where are you from?" The words sounded more like a snarl than a question.

"We're peasants from Hunan and have come to try our fortune in the city," Old Lin said.

The scarred man let his eyes rest on each of the four as if reading the truth in their faces and postures. Without warning, his hand flashed out and he grabbed Mei-hua's arm in an iron grip. Almost at the same time, he stepped back, pulling her with him. She stumbled, pain shooting up her arm as he twisted it in his attempt to hold her in front of him. As she righted herself to ease the pain, she rocked back against his chest. Before she had time to turn away again, the man pressed something cold and sharp against her throat.

"Don't lie to me, old man!" The knife pressed deeper into Mei-hua's neck. "Give me your silver or you'll be minus one gran'daughter!"

CHAPTER 6

MEI-HUA KNEW they were helpless. She couldn't see how they would escape. If they only lost their money, they would be lucky. This stretch of the road was lonely. It was almost night, and the peasants had already abandoned their fields until tomorrow. No one was likely to come along.

She glanced at Old Lin. With a micro-shake of his head he signaled her to do nothing. Not that she had much choice.

For their party to survive, these men must believe they were simple folk traveling to improve their lives. Not so unusual at the beginning of this new era. The bandits certainly must never suspect she was a magistrate's daughter. Such knowledge would make her too tempting to abduct for ransom. Chen Du and Nanny remained on the cart, still and pensive.

"Money! Give us your silver!" the thief yelled.

Old Lin looked at his charge, anguish in his eyes.

Mei-hua flashed him a look she hoped he would understand: turn the money over to the thieves. The money wasn't important. If he didn't turn it over, and they searched him, which Mei-hua was certain they would, they would kill him in anger.

Old Lin understood what she wanted. Bowing before the robber, he said, "Sir, I beg you to forgive me. I did try to mislead you, but clearly you are too clever."

The bandit leader drew himself up and shot a smug look at his men who all nodded in satisfaction.

"My Master charged me with taking his servants and cart to his father's home. However, I am but an old man and not able to challenge one such as you."

"You're right there, *old man*," the leader snarled back.

"Nevertheless, you are wrong when you believe I have any silver."

Before he could say more, the brute pulled Mei-hua closer to him; holding her in a tighter grip; and changing the position of the knife slightly, as if getting ready to cut her throat.

"Sir," Old Lin called out, raising his hands to stop him. "It is true we have no silver, however," he plunged his right hand deep into his left sleeve and pulled out a packet wrapped in a plain material, "I do have a small sum of money which I was taking as a..."

Again, he didn't have a chance to finish his sentence before a small, wiry man snatched the packet from his hand. He tore it open, tossed the cloth away, and with a triumphant gesture, he held up a string of copper coins to show their leader.

"Good. That's good," the leader said. Still gripping Mei-hua, he thrust his head toward the other three would-be peasants and growled, "Tie 'em up," to the men standing near him.

He tied Mei-hua's hands behind her back with rope and then, picking up the discarded cloth, he blindfolded her.

During all this Mei-hua never uttered a sound. She had to maintain the illusion of her muteness and, with it, her identity as an uneducated farm girl.

"Stand 'em on the side of the road, facing the fields," the leader called out to his men. "Okay, now!"

Mei-hua heard three thumps and then slumping sounds. She guessed her faithful servants had been struck, probably on the head, to knock them out.

"Push him over! You can't leave him lying in the road! He'll attract attention!" the leader called out. Then, pulling Mei-hua away, he said to her, "And we don't want anyone attracting attention, do we?"

He laughed, but the humor was lost on her. Abruptly, he stopped. He picked her up and roughly dropped her into the cart.

"Your family wanted us to use this cart, so we're taking it along," he guffawed again as he swung up into the driver's seat.

Mei-hua remained silent.

"What's the matter? Too scared to talk?" The angry scar on his neck danced up and down. "Well, you should be!"

"Boss, what are we going to do with her? She's too skinny to be able to do much work."

"Shut up! I have a plan. We have these copper coins, and a cart and ox to sell. Why not sell her off as well? She will bring good money." Again his harsh laugh, followed by snickering from the others.

Sell her off? Where to? For what? Would she become an indentured servant, practically a slave? She forced back the tide of terror threatening to once again overwhelm her. The burning jade added to her sense of urgency. Willing herself not to think about what might happen if she was sold, she struggled to concentrate, to make a plan of escape.

Soon the men stopped bragging about their "find" and fell silent as they continued walking, keeping pace with the slow cart. There was no way of knowing how much time had passed, but she sensed the sun had set because the air had become much colder. The abrupt movement of the cart knocked her shoulder against its hard side. The screeching wheels struck her very core, hurting her ears. Sleep was impossible. She did the only thing she could: wait.

After what seemed like hours, the cart no longer lurched violently from side to side as its wheels rolled through the worn country road's deep depressions. Mei-hua noticed its surface became smoother, as if better maintained. They must have entered a town. Could it be Hangzhou?

The cart stopped.

"Take that thing off her," commanded the leader.

As the blindfold fell from Mei-hua's eyes, she found herself on a narrow street with a long row of buildings running on either side for as far as she could see. The street was so narrow the cart would have prevented anyone from passing. If anyone had been there. Unfortunately, the hour was late and no one was around.

"Don't yell. If you do...," the leader held up a large square hand as if to strike her. He did not need to finish his sentence. She was only too aware of what he meant.

Mei-hua bowed her head in submission. She remained silent, but by now her earlier emotions of fear had turned to a burning anger. The jade remained hot against her skin. She drew a deep breath, centering her thoughts. The same strong, low voice from earlier, spoke to her, "In warfare, the superior warrior out-thinks the enemy."

What does that mean? She wondered. She was no warrior, although—as her father said—she may be in a war. Still, the words *out-think the enemy*, kept reverberating. She cast a fleeting glance around her. Her survival was up to her. And she would survive. She will out-think the enemy. While remaining standing in a humble slouch, she steeled her will and focused on what she needed to do to stay alive.

"Bring her here," he ordered his men. The wiry one directed another member of the gang to drag her off the cart and carry her into the building.

Once inside, Mei-hua examined the hovel, the only word she could think of to describe the room around her with its dirt floor and old, decaying walls of sticks partially covered with clay. There was little in the room besides a pile of rags in the corner and a couple of poorly made stools standing near an unventilated cooking fire.

"Ma! Hey, Ma! Look what I brought back!" the leader called into the room.

"What're you doing, bothering me in the middle of the night?" a high-pitched, penetrating voice demanded. It came from the pile of rags in the corner.

"Come on, Ma. This was a good night. Look at what I brought back," the leader said.

The rags moved. An apparition, like a ghost from the stories Mei-hua loved to hear, started to rise up. Soon, a grizzled old woman with long, loose, snarled hair appeared out of the rag pile.

"Well, where is it? Did you get gold or silver? What

is so important you had to tear your poor, old mother out of her sleep? Dummy, don't you know you coulda put my soul in danger? What if it was wandering about when you called me? I would have died! No soul! Do you wanna kill your mother!"

Even in the darkened room, watching this angry, strange creature screaming at the bandit leader, Mei-hua could see the gaps in her mouth where teeth were missing. The stress of the past many hours finally came to a head and something inside her snapped. Suddenly, she wanted to laugh. The scene of this crazed woman and her brutal son struck Mei-hua as a theatrical joke and not real life. She concentrated on maintaining a blank face.

Holding the small lantern he had used to light their way through the night, he let a shaft of light fall across Mei-hua. "Look, along with a cart and ox, I captured this."

The wizened woman walked stiffly over to the girl. She stood with her face within inches of Mei-hua's, carefully looking her over, breathing heavily. Her breath's foul odor jarred Mei-hua back to her senses. She no longer felt giddy

"What's your name," the old woman asked in a wheezing voice.

Mei-hua did not answer.

"I said, 'What's your name?'" she screamed, saliva spraying over Mei-hua's face.

Fighting to remain calm and in control, Mei-hua bowed her head silently, as if in submission. Suddenly, she was knocked off balance by a blow to the side of her head.

"She asked you your name! Answer her!" the bandit leader growled, his hand raised to strike her again.

Mei-hua fell to her knees as if begging forgiveness of the old woman, but she remained silent.

"You fool! You have brought home a mute! Don't you know she is bad luck! How did I ever raise such a stupid son?" his mother yelled.

"No. No. It is all right," her son insisted. "Listen, this is my plan. We are not keeping her. If she is bad luck, she will take it somewhere else. I will sell her to Old Yuan on Peace Street. She can work for him. He will pay a good price. I am sure of it."

"Old Yuan? The head of the beggars' guild? What will he do with a mute girl?"

"Well, look at her. She's skinny and pathetic looking. She just needs a special affliction and people will feel sorry for her and give her money. She can make lots for Old Yuan! All we have to do is, well, maybe break her legs. She would not be able to walk, only crawl along the streets."

"Yeah, Ben-ji is right! A young girl cripple. What a beggar! People would certainly throw money at such a pitiful sight. This girl would be worth a lot to Old Yuan, and that would mean she is worth something to us," the lean, short man standing against the wall, spoke out for the first time.

"Break her legs?" the old woman said in her shrill voice, ignoring the latest comment.

"Yeah! She would be a sorry sight! I will do it right now and we could sell her to Old Yuan today," her son replied, moving toward Mei-hua.

CHAPTER 7

BEN-JI'S MOTHER stepped in front of him as he began to move toward Mei-hua. Flinging her hand high into the air, she managed to slap her son on the side of his head.

"Idiot! You cannot break her legs! She will be worthless to us!"

"But, Ma, I just explained..."

"Explained! Explained! How would you live without me?" she said, her saliva sputtering through the air. "Sure, she'll be crippled if you break her legs, but so what! She is mute! People will step around her—even over her. She cannot call out to them, force them to notice her. Rich people step over corpses and never notice. Without a voice she is no more than a lump on the street."

The force of her logic managed to penetrate his mind. For a moment, he squeezed his eyes shut as if in thought.

"But then what? Are we stuck with a useless girl?" he asked, glaring at Mei-hua.

Even as Mei-hua bridled at being called "a useless girl," the realization that they wouldn't try to cripple her filled her with relief. Within seconds, however, relief turned to anger and shame as she recognized her own powerlessness. Her future was in the hands of these brutal strangers. Whatever they wanted to do, or not do, they could. The very first time her father gave her a serious task, something of great importance, she failed. Maybe she was useless after all.

At the thought of her father, her hand moved to the amulet he'd given her. She paused. The jade no longer burned but rested with a comforting warmth against her chest. *What'd this change mean?* she wondered. Her situation remained dire. Perhaps the jade wasn't warning her about danger after all. But then, why did it change temperature? Was it telling her she was safer, yet not quite safe? It was like learning a new language but without a tutor. Her attention turned back to her immediate problems.

She shook her head. The amulet did not matter now; magic would not rescue her here. She would have to do that herself.

Fortunately, unlike other young ladies born into wealthy families, Mei-hua had trained in the martial arts. Old Lin taught her. Though now well into his 60s and appearing fragile, his skill was famous throughout the region. Almost from the time she could talk, Mei-hua had begged her father to let the old master teach her. Her father finally relented and she started training under Old Lin. She studied hard, learned quickly, and had always been proud of her abilities. Yet, here she was: held captive once she ventured beyond her father's protective circle. Knowing that even Old Lin had not been able to save her from the unexpected knife at her throat did nothing to console her sense of failure.

Secretly, she examined the room. There was no other door. The only way out was the door they had come in, and the small, wiry sidekick to Ben-ji blocked the exit. There was one window: a small shuttered space near the door. She had no choice but to sit this out and wait for an opportunity to escape. If one ever came.

Mei-hua remained sitting on the hard-packed dirt floor, head down, but aware of what everyone was doing. The men lounged around the floor, too, filling the tight space. Ben-ji paced, and his mother, with a fingertip resting in her mouth, stood staring at her.

Without a word, the wizened creature came over and slowly walked around Mei-hua, poking her, jerking her head first one way then another, all the while examining her.

"Open your mouth!" she commanded. Mei-hua complied immediately. The old woman grabbed her jaw in an iron grip and began pushing on her teeth, as if testing their strength. The taste of sour, filthy fingers caused Mei-hua to gag, but she managed, with great concentration, to not vomit. She did not move or make a sound.

The creature stood back and again inspected Mei-hua from a distance.

"Well," she said glancing at her son, "this one has a certain style. She might be good as a servant." She shot a hand out, finger pointed at Mei-hua, and ordered, "Bow! Bow down before me."

At her command, Mei-hua fell to the floor. She gracefully dropped to her knees and stretched out flat on the floor, arms extended toward the woman, doing a full kowtow. Once completely flattened out, Mei-hua ignored the smell of dust and dirt as she knocked her head on the compact earthen floor several times. She guessed the old crone would not expect her to perform the complete formal kowtow, and Mei-hua hoped to impress her with her ability to do it and do it well.

"Look at that! What did I tell you? She has got style!" the old woman cried. "Yes. We can get good money for her." She turned around toward her son with glee. "When I visited my customer Madam Wu a couple days ago, she told me she wanted a new maid for her daughter." Pausing, she licked her cracked lips. "This one will fit her needs."

"But, Ma, she will never want this useless girl. She cannot speak; she is cursed." He spat on the floor. The slimy, thick glob landed inches from Mei-hua's knees. Startled, she jerked her worn pants back. Ben-Ji laughed.

"And how can you tell if this stupid girl knows anything about working in a big house? Without a tongue she cannot tell us what work she has done," he said.

"Never mind. She does not have to. Even if she is dim-witted, that is not our problem."

She encircled Mei-hua once more. "All I have to do is convince Madam Wu she is a rare, useful find. Once I have the money for her, I do not care what happens. And," she waved a hand over Mei-hua, "this one presents well enough for me to do my magic and convince Madam Wu to pay me top dollar! I can sell anything," she boasted.

Satisfied she had solved the problem of getting rid of the girl, the old woman continued, speaking to her prisoner and all of the men, "Now lie down. We cannot leave until morning, so we might as well get some sleep."

Mei-hua looked around again, this time more slowly. Where were they expected to sleep? The old woman herself had been sleeping in a pile of rags.

"Go ahead! Go to sleep," Ben-ji yelled at Mei-hua. "Take that corner," he indicated an area farthest from the door. Without another word, he settled down in front of the door with his men.

Mei-hua rose. Obviously, no one intended to offer her anything to sleep on or cover with, not even ragged bedding. The men all bedded down on the barren floor as if their sleeping arrangements were normal. After gazing over at the bandit group, she stepped quickly to the spot in the corner Ben-Ji had pointed out. Truth to tell, being ignored provided her with a moment of peace. She dropped down close to the wall, facing out into the room. Within moments, exhaustion pushed Mei-hua into a deep sleep.

A young woman, in worn, thread-bare clothing, knelt over a large wooden tub. Her arms thrust deep into the tub's cold water; she vigorously scrubbed a heavy pile of laundry. All the while a demonically grinning woman screamed at her, "Go faster! Do more, you lazy, worthless girl!" The servant girl nodded and turned toward her cruel mistress.

With a start, Mei-hua recognized the girl. It was her. She jolted awake and rose up onto her elbows. An acrid smell of old food, mixed with an overlay of stifling dust, assaulted her. Confused, she peered around. The sight of a bleak room remained, confounding her for another moment. Where was she? Why was she on a dirt floor? What was that snoring? What happened to Nanny?

Gradually, painfully, she began to remember.

"So, you are awake now, are you?" a voice rasped.

Mei-hua turned toward the questioner. A shriveled old woman's features appeared out of the darkness. Remembering what had happened and where she was, Mei-hua cast her eyes down and nodded in response, ever the compliant mute peasant.

"Eat this," the woman said as she handed over a chipped, stained bowl of cold rice soup.

Mei-hua took the plain, congee soup. With both hands wrapped around it, she started to bring it up to her mouth to drink when a small insect in the center of the bowl caught her eye. It struggled against the white liquid, fighting for its life. She blanched. However, realizing this may well be her only meal of the day—and hungry from not having eaten last night—Mei-hua carefully removed the insect, releasing it on the floor.

The old woman snorted, "Pretty particular, eh?"

"Yeah, you should have eaten that. It may be the only meat you will get in a long time!" Ben-Ji, standing over them, broke in with a smirk. He straightened out the disheveled jacket he'd slept in, before adding, "Never turn down food." He grinned again.

"Eat, Son," his mother ordered passing another bowl over to him. "You boys, too," she added to the other waking men.

"Ben-ji, I want you and the boys to accompany me down the river to Hangzhou and to Madam Wu's. I don't want anything to happen to our investment. There are too many thieves on the streets today. Not like it used to be when a woman could walk in safety," she said, disapproval ringing in her voice.

After a brief, harsh warning to Mei-hua to behave, the band set out. At the river bank hundreds of small sampans—long, narrow, flat bottomed boats—clogged the harbor. The band walked swiftly along the bank and soon came to a sampan seemingly identical to all the others around it. Without pausing, they jumped aboard and immediately shoved Mei-hua into the small wooden room projecting from its center. The room, built to protect passengers and boatpeople in bad weather, became Mei-hua's cell. With Ben-ji handling the oars at the front, and his mother and men guarding the hapless girl, they set off, traveling north.

By this time, the river had widened considerably in the flat lands of Zhejiang province, becoming sluggish. The inert delta forced Ben-ji to apply himself to his rowing. Considering the amount of river traffic and the river's resistance, they made remarkably good time getting to Hangzhou City.

Docking, Ben-ji, his mother, and the men stopped to buy a bowl of noodles. Although Mei-hua's stomach growled from hunger, they offered her nothing. While slurping down their dinner, the old woman instructed the men to stay with the sampan. She and Ben-ji would take the girl into the city.

After a short walk, they came to an enormous white wall, with a massive stone gate. They had arrived at Hangzhou. If the circumstances had been different, Mei-hua would have been excited to be here. As it was, she was happy only in the knowledge that at least now she knew where she was.

Along with scores of others, they passed through the immense, yawning doors of the city's gate, moving unnoticed right by a cluster of soldiers. Ben-ji kept a close grip on her arm as if helping her walk, giving Mei-hua no means of escape despite the nearness of soldiers and police. Even if she could have called out for help, she sadly thought, the only people who could have helped her were the very men she wanted to avoid. After all, she had gotten into this mess because she was on the run from the emperor and his agents until her family name was cleared.

Once inside the city walls, Mei-hua quickly lost track of where they were. Not only were the streets a dizzying maze, she was also overwhelmed and astounded at the towering buildings around her. While most streets weren't much more than alleyways, the houses looming on either side were multi-storied wooden structures. Each building tightly tucked in next to its neighbor. And, although it was the afternoon hour of rest, the streets bustled with people rushing about, buying and selling. How different from her old home with its single story houses and sunlit streets!

Staring at the crush of people surrounding them, Mei-hua thought they provided the perfect opportunity to get away.   It would be easy to lose her captors among such a crowd. She had to escape or she would be sold and live the rest of her life as a virtual slave. Looking around, she almost smiled. But how was she going to get Ben-ji to loosen his grip on her arm?

As Mei-hua considered how to get away, she heard the low, richly resonant ringing of gongs. The sound slowly became louder as if moving towards them. The gongs warned people to clear a path. Someone important was coming. As if by magic, the swarm of bodies—which only moments before clogged every bit of space—separated, leaving an opening in the middle of the street. Soon, several smartly dressed soldiers marched through carrying flags and other signs of public office. Next, an official government palanquin, resting on the shoulders of four heavily muscled men, moved past with imposing dignity. The palanquin's drawn curtains prevented her from seeing who was inside. Finally, another group of soldiers followed. The crowd closed behind the final pair of marching soldiers, reclaiming and again filling in every inch of road.

During this procession, Ben-ji never loosened his grip for an instant, even as the press of people shoved them against a shop front. At times the strain of the crowd forcing her in one direction and Ben-ji pulling her in another made her feel as if her arm could be wrenched out of its socket. Then, just after the official passed, an enormous man with a long beard put his hand on Ben-ji's shoulder. Ben-ji froze in place.

"Well, if it isn't my old friend, the stupid one," the huge man said, smiling down into Ben-ji's anxious face.

Clearly surprised at meeting this giant, Ben-ji momentarily loosened his grip on Mei-hua, but not enough for her to escape.

"Da Shan! How good to see you again," Ben-ji cried; his voiced cracked.

"What do you have there?" the big man asked, nodding toward Mei-hua.

"A young charge I am taking to Madam Wu," returned Ben-ji's mother. She had been separated by the crowds, and had just managed to push through to get back to her son and Mei-hua.

At the sight of her, Da Shan's manner became polite and non-threatening. Nevertheless, after exchanging greetings, he turned his attention back to Ben-ji.

"Where is my money?" he demanded.

"You know you will get it. I always pay my debts," Ben-ji said, his mouth twitching uncontrollably.

"Not if you can avoid it," the other returned.

"What money? What debts?" demanded the old woman.

"He is not a lucky gambler, Madam Yang," the big man said. "He owed me money, but still I was foolish enough to give him credit for another game. He lost that game, too. I have been patient. Now I want my money."

"How much does he owe?" she asked.

When Da Shan told her, she tried not to betray her surprise, although her face lost its color.

"But don't worry," Da Shan said, looking hard at Mei-hua. "I know how you can repay me in full."

"Nonsense! What would you do with a child?" the old woman said.

"What are you going to do with the child?" he returned. "She should fetch a bit as a bondservant, I should think."

He reached out for Mei-hua. Just as his hand was about to close over her free arm, the old woman cried out to her son, "Kick him! Keep him away!"

Ben-ji reacted instantly to his mother's command. Dropping his grip on Mei-hua, he pushed her out of Da Shan's reach. At the same time, he gave the giant a ferocious kick in the shin. As the two began to fight, Mei-hua pressed quickly through the crowd already forming to watch this new entertaining sight.

Rounding a corner, she ran several more blocks, turned another corner, then stopped to catch her breath. She didn't know where she was, but at least she was free.

"You are going the wrong way," a sharp voice said from behind her.

Mei-hua knew who it was even before she saw the wizened face. Her stomach dropped. Glancing up the street, she prepared to run again.

How could she have been so fast? Mei-hua thought.

"Do not try to escape from me, little one," the old

woman said. "I know this city. You do not. Without me your fate could very well be much worse than being a bondservant in a big house. They will feed you, clothe you. Out here on the streets, no one cares if you starve. You cannot escape; do not try," she repeated.

Mei-hua was aware of the jade's renewed heat against her skin. It seemed to amplify the crone's fateful words.

CHAPTER 8

MEI-HUA BENT HER HEAD in submission to the old woman's will. This time she was not acting. She had lost again, and she knew it. Whether in cities or rural areas, it was impossible to survive on one's own. No one trusted a person without ties to other human beings. Even beggars belonged to guilds. The guilds became their family: they organized the beggars, told them what to do, and gave them protection, support, and guidance. At the moment Mei-hua was worse than a beggar. She was alone.

Those without family or friends suffered the hardest and meanest of lives. For all she knew, her trusted servants were dead somewhere along the road. She had no idea what had happened to her father. She didn't want to think he might be in jail waiting to die for crimes he didn't commit, but she knew it was possible, even likely. And this false criminal charge put her entire family—including herself—in mortal danger.

The old woman was right; being a bondservant wasn't the worst thing that could happen to a young girl without family or friends.

As she bowed her head, however, she also began planning on how she could use her position as a servant to learn more about the city and its citizens. She may even find her father's old friend. If only he had mentioned his friend's name to her! Still, as she thought about it, she remembered certain details about the man she was to stay with. He had become friends with her father because they were alike in several ways: they were both Southerners, about the same age, had studied together, and took their critical, final examinations at the same time. They both passed in the top one percent. As a result, their names were put in a pool of men considered competent to hold government office. The Imperial Court immediately appointed each of them to government positions. Moreover, her father's friend had a family. No name, true, but perhaps enough detail to find him once she learned more about Hangzhou. How many people could fit this description?

The old woman cackled with delight, believing Mei-hua had surrendered. "Come along now. This will be useful for both of us: You will have a safe home, and I will have a lot of money."

Without trying to escape again, Mei-hua followed the wizened woman through the back streets. The building fronts spanned several times more than the 10–12 foot wide homes and shops they passed earlier. Impenetrable walls pushed up against the street, signaling that they had reached a wealthy district. Behind the high walls, sprawling, sumptuous homes and gardens lay hidden from the dirt and noise of the congested street.

Finally, turning a corner, they found themselves in front of an impressive gate with colorful, human-sized, door god statues on either side of the entrance. Their ferocious expressions and fighting stances kept evil spirits from entering the house. As she cast a quick glance at the brightly painted warrior gods, Mei-hua thought about how well they must protect the family behind the wall. What demons would dare challenge them?

A broad sign hung high over the door, its deeply engraved characters inlaid with gold. Mei-hua struggled to read it but couldn't. The old woman hurried her along, keeping close to the building's wall.

They walked along for two full blocks before turning right. Soon, they came to a small, plain, worn wooden door in the impenetrable wall. Servants and peddlers used this entrance. Usually, in such wealthy homes, only important guests, as well as family and friends, entered through the high front gate with its richly carved double doors. The old woman stopped and, after patting down her clothing to make herself more presentable, took a rock from the street and banged it against the door.

A middle-aged man wearing immaculate white pants and a long indigo tunic opened the door several inches and peered out. Seeing two women dressed in rumpled, plain clothing, he abruptly asked what they wanted.

"Honorable sir," the old woman began in an overly sweet, singsong voice, "I am Madam Yang and have come a long distance to see Madam Wu."

After another disdainful glance at the two in front of him, he grimaced and, without a word, began to close the door in their faces.

The old woman, holding her hands respectfully in front of her, quickly added, "who is expecting us." She nodded her head slightly in Mei-hua's direction. "I have brought her a much needed servant."

The man paused. He examined Mei-hua as if he were calculating her worth as a servant. After a few seconds, he pulled back, still dissatisfied. She had not passed his test, whatever that had been.

The old woman stepped forward before he could shut the door and, in an urgent voice, started talking again. "Sir, I must apologize for our appearance, but I wanted to bring her here as soon as possible. We have had to travel a great distance to find and bring this girl for Madam Wu." She paused, dropped her eyes and shook her head as if explaining a difficult problem. Then, with an obsequious glance at the door keeper, she continued. "You may think I am a fool. That there are many girls in the city and this was an easy task, but no, not so easy. Madam Wu was quite particular. Her requirements forced me to search far and wide for just the right maid. Naturally, as soon as I found her, I rushed here without even changing into more proper clothing."

The look of suspicious distrust never left his eyes, but the door keeper decided to err on the side of caution. After all, what if his mistress did know this creature? Finally, he allowed the old woman to convince him Madam Wu expected them. With an impatient flick of his hand, he opened the door wide and motioned for them to come inside the compound.

"Stay here," he said. He called a young servant over and told him to alert their mistress that Madam Yang and her charge had arrived.

Shortly, the boy returned, saying to send them in. The gate keeper sullenly escorted the old woman and Mei-hua across the compound garden to an interior door. There he left them in the hands of a young female servant who guided them to the rooms of their Mistress.

As they entered Madam Wu's room, Mei-hua looked around and a strong sense of homesickness overtook her. The longing for home was so strong she could taste it. The elegance and beauty of the room reminded her of her own rooms at home with her father. On an ornate wood table, translucent white porcelain vases sat near a carved flower of multicolored jade. A large scroll hung on a nearby wall. It depicted a family, an elderly couple on a raised platform, a young man kneeling in front of them, and a young woman standing off to one side holding a plate of food. Mei-hua knew the painting; it came from the famous book *Filial Piety*. It was a reminder of how the younger generation was to care for their parents. Another scroll hanging nearby had a couplet on the merits of virtue over beauty in a wife.

Certainly the details varied, and this house's decorations were much more lavish than her home. Nevertheless, a sense of the familiar almost stopped her breathing. She had lost so much! Would she ever be safe and happy in her own home with her father again?

Several beautifully attired maid servants stood about, ready to assist their mistress and her guest, another woman of similar age and bearing.

Madam Wu welcomed the ancient woman as a good friend. "Madam Yang, please come in and sit! Madam Fei and I are having tea. Join us." With a delicate flutter of her hand, she indicated a place across from her distinguished looking guest, who gazed steadily at the old woman.

Madam Yang oozed politeness and friendliness. "Madam Wu, you are much too kind. I am sorry to have bothered you without giving notice."

"Nonsense. We are only too happy to have you join us."

Mei-hua wondered that Madam Wu didn't recognize her captor's act as one of a snake charmer. Still, she also maintained the fiction and acted like an obedient servant, standing quietly and meekly behind the old woman. She was so intense in observing her new surroundings that she was only mildly aware of her amulet hanging coolly around her neck.

After enjoying a cup of tea and asking about each other's health, the old woman delicately brought up the topic of Madam Wu's wanting a maid. Speaking about money or business was not considered polite, even though it was what brought this odd couple together. The old woman approached the idea of selling a maid into Madam Wu's service with care. At the same time, Madam Wu, who was well aware the old woman had brought a maid to sell, also avoided a direct conversation about buying the girl.

A good wife in a wealthy family never went shopping or investigating outside of the walls of her home. She relied completely on less affluent women, who had more freedom of movement, to shop for her. Madam Yang was just such a woman and she had a reputation for finding whatever the ladies behind the walls needed—whether jewelry, silk, or even indentured servants. Once more, Madam Wu sincerely enjoyed the old one's presence because she also brought gossip about other houses in the city. Without her, the isolated wealthy women would never know what was happening outside their strong, firm walls.

As a matter of fact, while Madam Wu appeared to take no note of the young girl, she obliquely scrutinized her. Mei-hua understood the rules of polite behavior, and she also understood that when money was involved, relationships had their own rules. She knew there would be serious negotiating over how much Madam Yang would get for Mei-hua. Knowing Madam Wu would try to pay the lowest price didn't bother her at all. A good and shrewd manager of the family money had to negotiate. It was her responsibility as keeper of the family budget. Besides, Mei-hua had immediately felt a kinship to this home and this kindly woman who sat entertaining Madam Yang.

There was no discussion over the cost of selling the girl to the Wu house, however. The old crone immediately announced she realized the girl's muteness appeared to be a serious flaw. She apologized for the bad fate which took the girl's voice away. Then, continuing in her singsong voice, she said: "Yet, you will find this girl an exceptional maid. She has many, many unique and priceless qualities. You can only understand them when you have had her working in your house. Take her as your maid and you will find her more than satisfactory. Besides, a maid who cannot speak is a rare blessing: she will never argue or spread family gossip," the old woman said.

To sweeten the deal, the old woman proposed leaving Mei-hua with her as a bondservant before they agreed upon a final contract. Never having heard of such a compromise, Madam Wu became intrigued. After a short time, the two women came to a temporary agreement. Mei-hua would remain in the house on a trial basis.

Turning to her other guest, Madam Wu asked, "Tell

me Madam Fei, what do you think about this young girl?"

Madam Fei, who observed the discussion, but had remained quiet, motioned for Mei-hua to come over and to kneel before her. After Mei-hua knelt down, Madam Fei looked deeply into her face and caressed her head. As a famous local fortune teller, Madam Fei read people's fates in their faces and head shapes. Did they have good or bad futures? All was laid out plainly for her to see.

"Ah-hah! This girl has extraordinarily lucky features. She will have an unusual and wealthy life. Even though she appears to be but a poor girl, fame and fortune will be hers!"

At this unexpected declaration of the mute girl's good fate, the other women murmured and nodded, while staring at her in open curiosity.

"Really?" Madam Wu looked at Mei-hua with interest. Then she said, "Come here, let me look at you more closely."

Mei-hua did as told. What luck; this could only help her. Nevertheless, she didn't believe in fortune telling, so discounted her prediction. Her father claimed fortune tellers told people only what they wanted to hear. Besides, how could she be lucky when she had already lost her family, her home, and her trusted servants? No, she didn't believe Madam Fei's prediction, but if it helped win a decent place to live while she searched out her father's friend, then it was all right with her.

After inspecting Mei-hua again, Madam Wu said, "Well, with such a good fortune, I must buy her. I am not at all sure how being mute will affect her work, but I don't want to go against fate." With this decision,

Madam Wu offered to pay over the market price to secure the maid.

The greedy woman's face wreathed in smiles at the suggestion. What a windfall! She immediately agreed. This was much more than she ever expected to get.

As soon as she received the silver, she excused herself, saying urgent business at home required her attention. In fact, she was afraid Madam Wu would change her mind and take the money back.

After the wizened woman left, the fortune teller turned toward her friend. "You did the right thing, Madam Wu. You'll not be sorry. Right now she looks pitiable, given her clothes and all, but her face is intelligent and comely."

The Mistress of the house nodded her head thoughtfully, "Yes, yes." Then, as if deciding on something, "You're right about the clothing. We must get rid of it immediately."

"Orchid," she said to one of the women sitting on the far side of her. "Come here and take this girl with you. She needs a more appropriate dress. She's about your size. She can wear your yellow dress until we can get something made for her."

Mei-hua shot a quick look over at the other women in the room and realized several of the young women sitting on the sides were not guests, but maids. She was surprised, not because they sat in their Mistress's presence, but because they all wore elaborate and beautiful silk dresses. In fact, even she never owned clothing as sumptuous as what these servants wore.

Her father encouraged moderation in her appearance. He wanted her to accent the development of her inner self, not her looks. While his views were unusual, especially for a girl child, she never questioned the truth of what he said. Without the influence of female relatives determining how she should behave, Mei-hua had a lot of freedom under her father's guidance. She grew up unencumbered by many of the constraints other girls experienced. Yet, when she saw these beautiful women and girls, and heard that she would also dress in the shimmering, soft silks, she could not hide the gleam in her eyes. Perhaps being a bondservant here wouldn't be so bad after all.

CHAPTER 9

MEI-HUA FOLLOWED Orchid out of the room, down a veranda, through a small gate and an adjacent court yard. The servants' area was off in a corner of the mansion. At first Orchid remained quiet. After they passed through the small gate, however, she relaxed and started talking.

"You're lucky to be coming into this house," she said glancing at the new girl. "The mistress is kind and the work is not hard. You're to be Ping-an's maid." Forgetting briefly that her audience was mute, she paused to give the girl a chance to comment. When Mei-hua only looked at her, Orchid quickly continued, "Ping-an's not as kind as her mother, the mistress, but she's not mean. You know what the five elements are?"

Mei-hua nodded. There were five elements in nature: fire, earth, wood, metal, and water. They explained why people acted the way they did. Every person's personality was made up of a combination of these elements, but one was always dominant.

Orchid went on, "She's a Fire personality in every way: she laughs and talks a lot at times, but she also gets anxious and feels overwhelmed quite easily. Still, she's just a child. You'll get used to her."

As Orchid chatted nonstop, Mei-hua took in her new surroundings. A number of antique porcelain bowls containing miniature trees or freshly cut flowers lined the veranda and adorned the courtyard. She decided this wasn't a merchant family because the house's classical decorations showed restraint in both beauty and style. From what she heard, wealthy merchants expressed more exuberance in their colors and decorations, even though the government tried to control them through sumptuary laws. These laws, which limited what families could have in their houses, and even what materials and colors they could wear, seldom worked. If people had money, they bought what they wanted, no matter what the law required.

From the appearances of the courtyard and the Mistress's room, Mei-hua deduced the father of this family had to be a high ranking government official. Pleased, she tucked away the thought that with such a family, she should be able to learn about other official families in the area through the gossip of the Mistress's visiting women friends. Her goal would be to pay close attention to their casual conversations. In this way, she'd discover which official in Hangzhou City was her father's friend. What she would do then, well, she would figure that out later.

Entering a simple bamboo structure, Orchid gave her a bucket and directed her to the well. Mei-hua understood she was to collect water to warm for a bath before she dressed. The citizens of Hangzhou were well-known for being particular about bathing and cleanliness.

She cheerfully went off to get water, secure in the idea she would be able to use this house to find her father's friend. While at the well, she surreptitiously removed her amulet and tucked it into her sleeve. With her mind only half on the task at hand, she returned carrying the bucket mostly filled with water. As she put it down on the floor, Orchid said, "Take it over to the drain and be quick about your bath. The Mistress doesn't like to be kept waiting."

Mei-hua's eyes opened wide in surprise. One bucket of water? How was she supposed to bathe with only one bucket?

"What's the matter with you? You can't expect to use up all the water. You're not the mistress, you know," Orchid chided. "There's plenty of water to wash your hair and clean up. Now hurry, we have to present you to the young mistress, too."

Mei-hua stared at the bucket, which looked awfully small to her now. With dismay, she also realized there was no fire to warm the water. Apparently, they were not going to waste wood to build a fire for heating a young bondservant's bath water. Her bath would be one bucket of cold well water.

There was nothing to do but make the best of it. With resignation and a slight shiver, she took up a bamboo dipper and began to pour water over her shoulder.

"Not so quick! If you wash like that, you won't have enough water to complete your bath! Where were you born, anyway? Don't you know how to wash?"

With a disgusted glance at the young girl, Orchid

grabbed the dipper out of her hand and proceeded to show her how to both wash her hair and take a complete bath with the single bucket of water. She filled a small dipper to make her hair and skin wet, then let Mei-hua scrub all over with soap and put some in her hair. With the remaining water, Orchid helped Mei-hua rinse away the soap.

"Now don't be so careless in the future. This is a big house and we all need baths. Hangzhou doesn't have water to waste, so neither do we. If there isn't enough water, you know who will suffer, don't you?" Orchid asked. Without pausing, she answered herself: "Right, us.

"I just wonder where you came from that you don't even know how to take proper care of yourself," she continued. "Do you know how to dress appropriately?" she asked.

Although offended by the question, Mei-hua realized Orchid was not being sarcastic but was sincerely concerned. After all, Mei-hua had on a simple pair of peasant pants and blouse when she came to the house, a far cry from the fine clothing worn by the maids of the house.

She felt the blood rise in her face. She was sure she was blushing. Being a bondservant was not going to be as easy as she thought. No one had ever spoken to her the way this servant woman did. Nor had anyone ever suggested that she, the daughter of an educated government official, didn't know the rudiments of cleanliness or dress. Her high spirits sank as she once again realized how alone and friendless her situation was. No one knew her or her family. She was nobody, nothing more than a human blob only fit to do...what? If the maid questioned her like this, how would the mistress ever accept her as a companion to her daughter? Where would she end up next?

Mei-hua dressed and once again hid her jade necklace under her blouse, savoring its coolness as it rested against her once more. Its presence gave her comfort, a sign of who she was and the family she belonged to. When she stepped out, clean, with her hair tied back, and dressed in Orchid's old, but elegant, yellow skirt and jacket, the older maid nodded with satisfaction.

After Orchid adjusted the thick brown ribbon holding up Mei-hua's skirt, she said, "Good. Now you are presentable. We can go back to the mistress."

Once they returned to Madam Wu's room, Ping-an was summoned. Nervous, Mei-hua hoped the child liked her; otherwise Madam Wu certainly would not keep her as a servant. In the past, she had played with younger cousins on their rare visits, but, as an only child, Mei-hua had limited experience with children. Now she wished she knew more about how to handle little ones. As she tried to think of how to entertain a young child, something, anything, to make the girl like her and want her as a maid, a clear, bell-like voice from outside the door announced her new mistress's arrival.

To Mei-hua's surprise, a dainty, well-dressed young woman of her own age entered the room. The girl leaned slightly on the arm of another older maid. Mei-hua took a quick, secretive glance at the girl's feet. Just as she thought, at each step and swish of the flowing, flowered silk skirt, the tiniest bound feet she had ever seen peeked out. Covered with brightly embroidered shoes in red, blue, and tan flowers, they matched the skirt and jacket this delicate creature wore. Considered cultured and beautiful, her crippled feet were too painful for the girl to constantly put her full weight on them. Without her maid, she would have difficulty walking.

Hiding both her surprise and disappointment at the age of the supposed child, Mei-hua behaved as much like the perfect maid as she could. At the same time, she was painfully aware of how this girl's age could prove to be a problem in carrying out her plan to examine the surroundings. Her young mistress would not only require more attention, she would also be more aware of what her maid did and where she went.

"Mother!" the girl cried out with a smile as she pulled a decorated comb out of the bun on her head. "Look what Aunt Xi sent to me!" She handed her mother a comb of white jade Mei-hua blossoms set on silver branches.

"Oh, a beautiful piece." Madam Wu said turning it over in her hand. "This is quite valuable, daughter; you must take great care with it." Then looking at the maid assisting Ping-an, she added, "Don't let her lose it. I'm holding you responsible."

The maid bowed, eyes on the floor. "Yes, ma'm," she murmured. Clearly, it was not unusual for the maid to be held accountable for Ping-an's actions.

As Madam Wu handed the ornament back to Ping-an, she said, "Daughter, I found a maid to be your companion." Madam Wu motioned for Mei-hua to come forward.

Quickly, Mei-hua stepped towards her. Ping-an watched her curiously as her fingertips played over the jade blossoms of her new comb.

"What's your name?" she asked the young maid.

Silent, Mei-hua stood with her head down.

"She can't tell you, daughter. The girl is mute."

In answer to Ping-an's questioning glance, her mother continued, "I'll tell you more later, but don't worry. You'll find her lack of speech isn't a problem. She'll serve you well. And she'll make a good listener," her mother added with a smile. "You don't need any more chatty servants, do you?"

The maid who had just received orders to watch over the hair ornament blushed. Ping-an nodded and laughed gaily.

"Since we don't know her name and she can't tell us what it is, let's name her ourselves," her mother said.

"Yes, a new name for her new place in our house," Ping-an agreed. "What shall we call her?"

Mei-hua watched Ping-an through veiled eyes, and thought her new young mistress must not be very clever if she had to ask her mother to help her devise a name. Did Ping-an rely on her mother to tell her everything?

"How about 'Mei-hua,' the name of the flowers on your new ornament," her mother suggested. "Since your other maids have flower names, this Mei-hua will go nicely in your flower garden," she said.

Ping-an clapped her hands in delight. "Perfect!"

Mei-hua, however, started at the name. Again she felt her face grow hot and flushed. What a coincidence that they chose her real name!

Noticing her face, Ping-an returned, "Or maybe Xiao-zhu, Little Pearl. That's also a common name." Ping-an looked mischievously at the new maid, while fingering the red silk ribbon hanging long and loose from her waist. *Zhu* also meant the color red. She was obviously making a joke at Mei-hua's expense.

At this comment, Mei-hua dropped her eyes so no one could see her anger flare up at being so rudely treated. Fortunately, with her eyes down she looked even more submissive to Madam Wu, who then gently scolded her daughter and told her to be kind to the new maid.

Undaunted, Ping-an cheerfully cried, "Never mind! Mei-hua, will be her name!"

After spending enough time with her mother to be polite, Ping-an asked to be excused. She told her mother she needed to study.

"Certainly. It's about time. Teacher Song says you are not doing very well. You must study and improve. Go along, and take your new maid with you."

A pout briefly crossed her daughter's face. "Yes, Mama." She turned to Mei-hua and Orchid. "Come along."

Leaning slightly on Mei-hua's arm, she minced slowly back in the direction of the gardens while Orchid and two other maids patiently followed close behind.

Ping-an told her new maid she had no intention of studying; she wanted to escape from her mother and show off to her brother. He would be so jealous. Now she had as many maids and servants as he had. His competitive spirit made him always want the most and best of everything. And, as the oldest and only boy in the family, their mother usually gave in to whatever he wanted.

A young man leaned against a pillar on the veranda surrounding the small garden in front of Ping-an's rooms. Mei-hua noticed that although he saw them come into the garden, he chose to ignore them. A frown marred his handsome features.

"Guei-lung! Come, see what I have!" Ping-an called out as they started down the veranda towards him.

"What?" he said as they came up to him. "You are so excited about getting a new maid. I should think you would be more mature than that." He sarcastically spit out the word "mature."

"Mother just found her for me," Ping-an went on as if not noticing his sarcasm.

"He's really jealous," she whispered to Mei-hua and then grinned.

"She's special. Isn't she lovely?" Ping-an said to her brother.

Guei-lung looked the new maid over. "She's ugly," he announced. "Look at her big feet!"

Mei-hua again had to fight to keep her temper down. Big feet, indeed! She remembered well when as a child her father's older sister had first tried to bind them. Foot binding made the girl's feet extremely tiny and, when hidden in exquisite embroidered silk shoes, they were considered beautiful. However, to make such tiny treasures required breaking toe bones and binding them under the foot. When complete, the girl lived with constant pain. And, as with Ping-an, if the binding creates the ideal three-inch size foot, she must have assistance to walk even a short distance since her feet could not support her.

When Mei-hua's father saw the big, silent tears running down her cheeks from the pain she suffered, his heart melted. In spite of warnings from his sister that his daughter would never find a husband if she had big feet, he insisted that his daughter's feet be allowed to grow naturally. After all, her mother, as a Uyghur woman, never had her feet bound, and he married her. Someone would marry Mei-hua he assured his unhappy sister.

After this, Mei-hua's father's government position moved him and his daughter further away from his sister and her family. Because of the distance, there were few visits from her aunt again. Thus ended all attempts to make Mei-hua conform to a feminine ideal. Her father was busy with work and often let her do whatever she wanted.

She couldn't stand Guei-lung's arrogance and rudeness. So now, in spite of her decision to be a well-behaved, subservient maid, Mei-hua defiantly stuck a foot out from under her long dress.

"Of course they're big," Ping-an tossed back, "she's a servant. She has to work. How could she work with lotus feet?" she asked.

Guei-lung looked hard into Mei-hua's face. "And her eyes are too round. Who knows what she's thinking? Even a baby can talk, but she can't."

As in any household, large or small, news traveled fast. He knew everything about the new maid, even before he'd seen her. After a pause, he added pointedly, "You know, with those eyes she might not even be a real Han." He threw in this last comment about his sister's new maid just to irritate Ping-an.

Sure enough, Ping-an reacted with anger. "Well, she's mute, that's certain, but to say she's not Han isn't fair! She's not a barbarian! You don't know anything! You're just jealous and so you're being nasty."

Guei-lung smiled. He'd won. Making Ping-an angry was so easy!

Mei-hua was stunned at Guei-lung's words. Not Han! What he'd guessed was partly true: her father was Han, but her mother wasn't. Although her mother had died during childbirth and Mei-hua never really learned much about her mother's people, she knew they did look different. In addition to having rounded eyes, they tended to be taller and more robust than the Han ideal. And, of course, the women didn't bind their feet. Although she didn't know much about her mother's people, her father taught her to be proud of both her Han and Uyghur heritage.

"You're a liar, Guei-lung!" Ping-an said loudly, raising her hand and stepping towards him.

Guei-lung opened his mouth in mock horror and covered his face with his arms as he stepped backward. Not looking behind him, he struck a pot full of dirty cleaning water left behind by one of the servants. His foot hit the pot and it went crashing onto its side. Gray liquid cascaded in a stream down the veranda.

"Now look at the mess you've made!" Ping-an yelled.

Just as she was about to say more to her brother, an elderly woman entered the garden. She had come to quiet their argument before their mother heard of it.

"Ping-an! Don't speak to your older brother that way," she snapped at the hapless girl. "You know better than to get into an argument with him!"

"And you, Guei-lung," she continued, turning on the young man, "you needn't smirk like that. What a way to talk! This bondmaid is mute, not deaf. Your mother would be very unhappy to learn of your treatment of a new servant."

"I'm sorry, Auntie Lao," the brother and sister said in unison. Aunt Lao was their father's oldest sister and, therefore, deserved their respect. Besides, they both liked the kindly elderly woman.

"I won't argue with Older Brother anymore," Ping-an added. She was ashamed of herself for trying to make him jealous.

"And what about you, Guei-lung?" the lady asked.

"I will not needlessly insult the servants," he said in apology, adding, "even if they don't know what I'm saying."

"Guei-lung!" his aunt said, chiding him again.

"What are we to do with you?"

With an impish grin he said, "I don't know, Auntie."

Aunt Lao tried to glare at him, but she was too fond of him to be cross. So, she merely scolded them mildly once more, told them to get a servant to clean up the mess Guei-lung made, then passed over the veranda and into their mother's courtyard.

Mei-hua didn't like Guei-lung. He insulted her and was rude. Still, she suspected his interference was unexpected good luck. His attitude toward her almost guaranteed that Ping-an would want to keep her on as a maid. The brother-sister rivalry was definitely good for her.

CHAPTER 10

GUEI-LUNG CALLED to two of the servants as he left his sister and strode off in the opposite direction. Ping-an watched him go. Turning to Orchid she nodded with a grin.

"I'll bet he's going to practice shooting his bow near the bamboo woods," she said. "Let's take Mei-hua over and introduce her to Guei-lung at work." She laughed and grabbed hold of Mei-hua's arm.

Mei-hua knew wealthy families groomed their sons for the most prestigious type of job in the country: being a government official. She was sure Guei-lung's parents were preparing him for this too. Such a position meant honor, status, and economic advancement for the whole family.

The Emperor demanded his officials be well-read and expert in the Confucian classics. However, having just taken back the government after more than one hundred years of foreign rule, he also wanted his officials trained in the use of weapons. In fact, candidates who wanted to join the government had to pass tests on their skills in archery and horsemanship. This was a marked change from the Yuan Dynasty's rule. Under the Mongol invaders, Han government officials were forbidden to have weapons; by law they only studied what was needed to run the civil bureaucracy. This did not include achieving military skills which could be used against their foreign rulers. However, when the Han Emperor established the Ming Dynasty, he insisted his officials be capable of defending, as well as administering, his government.

While Ping-an and her maids stood talking, they saw Guei-lung's servant hurry past, going toward the bamboo woods carrying a bow and a quiver of arrows.

"Come. I'll get back at Guei-lung for making fun of my new maid." She turned toward Mei-hua. "He has to practice his bow each week, but he's terrible! We'll pretend we are going for a walk and watch him. He'll be so embarrassed!" She giggled gaily as she swirled her skirt. The quick twirling movements almost made her lose her balance. Orchid immediately reached out and steadied the girl. Ping-an leaned into the trusted maid's arm while her silver laugh continued to light up the garden.

"You should go to your rooms and study, as you told your Mother you would," Orchid said. Being older, as well as responsible for her mistress, she tried to gently discourage this escapade, which could easily lead her young charge into trouble again. Auntie Lao might return, and Orchid would be held accountable for the siblings' mischief, not Ping-an and Guei-lung. But it was no use. Ping-an had made up her mind.

"It isn't far," Ping-an said as they helped her along.

"Guei-lung always practices near the gate where there is a long, straight walk. The rest of the path through the woods is too curvy for shooting a bow."

The bamboo wood's gate was near and the group of young women moved at a leisurely pace. Mei-hua and Orchid supported Ping-an from either side as she delicately stepped along. Mei-hua, used to more activity, grumbled silently to herself. Carrying her mistress would be easier than shuffling down the path at such a snail's pace. Finally, they covered the short distance and reached the entrance to the bamboo grove; they stood outside, silently listening.

Twong. Twong. They heard Guei-lung's arrows fly from his bow.

"Open the gate, Lily," Ping-an ordered another of her maids. "Quietly," she added, with a grin of expectation.

As the small wooden door swung open, Ping-an entered with her maids. They came up behind Guei-lung just as he let another arrow fly. The arrow missed its mark by several inches.

"I believe you do need more practice," Ping-an said. Putting on a serious expression, she pursed her lips and bobbed her head thoughtfully.

Guei-lung whirled around in surprise. He guffawed at seeing his sister and her maids. Mei-hua thought he would still try arguing with Ping-an, but his mood seemed to have changed entirely. Suddenly, Mei-hua was conscious of how good-looking he was: black smiling eyes under thick eyebrows, a straight nose and, yes, an engaging laugh.

"Well, it's good to see you! This calls for a break!" he said pushing back a stray tuft of hair falling over his forehead. "I hate all this practicing," he added as he signaled to the servants.

Responding to his waving hand, the servants brought a table into the garden and put it in a small pavilion built on the side of the path. Several maids left, returning shortly with tea and sweet rice cakes.

Ping-an sank down thankfully next to the table, tucking her lotus feet in a ladylike manner under the folds of her diaphanous skirt. She adjusted the sleeves of her jacket and rested her elbows on the table. In spite of her mischievous side, clearly she had little strength and easily tired. Mei-hua frowned slightly. The bound feet limited her activities, making it difficult for her to be strong in body, in spite of her spirited nature.

After munching on sweet cakes, Guei-lung suggested they all play a board game.

"What will be the punishment for the one who loses?" Lily asked.

"We'll give them a word and they have to make up a two line poem using it," Guei-lung said.

Everyone agreed and the game began. Mei-hua didn't play. People still treated her as if she were not very bright because she was mute. It didn't bother her. Standing behind Ping-an, her mind was free to observe and think.

Ping-an was the first to lose.

"How about if I sing a song instead of making up a poem?" she asked.

Guei-lung smirked. "You can't cheat. We agreed. You must do a poem," Guei-lung said. "And you have to use the words *da jiao* in it."

Mei-hua stared angrily at Guei-lung. *Da jiao* meant "big foot."

Ping-an's face reddened as she caught Mei-hua's angry glance at her brother. "Guei-lung! You're not being polite! Auntie Lao told you to be nicer to the maids!" Ping-an replied heatedly.

"You misunderstand me, dear sister. I didn't mean 'big foot.' I meant 'great understanding.' You know that both of these phrases sound the same." He looked up at Mei-hua with a smile and a shrug of his shoulders. "I can't help it if you are always getting things mixed up," he said as if talking to his sister.

Mei-hua knew he was baiting her, just as he did Ping-an. She lightly rested her hand over her father's amulet as it lay warm and hidden under her clothing. As she put her hand over it, she heard a calm, deep voice murmur, "A quick temper can lead to foolish action and the road to ruin."

By now she had begun to recognize this voice which appeared to arise from inside her head. The jade was giving her guidance from the ancient philosopher, Sun Tzu. Sun Tzu was a favorite of her father's and he insisted she study Sun Tzu's writings because he was both an educated man and a brilliant military leader. Talents needed for the new world they found themselves in.

A quick temper, a rash rush to anger. Yes, Guei-lung was goading her and she fell for it. Now directing the rising irritation at herself for her own folly and gullibility, she gave a small, almost imperceptible, shake of her head. She'd never let Guei-lung provoke her again. This was all a game to him, but to her there were more important things to think about. She would not allow herself to get sidetracked by his pettiness. It needlessly used up her mental and emotional energy. Her life had turned upside down in a matter of a few days. Would she be able to cope with it? She steeled her heart and only hoped she could stay on track.

As Guei-lung looked at Mei-hua with his teasing eyes, she maintained a bland, neutral face. Instead of showing irritation or anger, she addressed him with a cool, distant, smile. The smile of one who is not involved.

Guei-lung seemed to notice the change and a brief questioning look passed over his face. He glanced back toward his sister and chortled again.

"Well, are you going to compose a poem or not?"

Ping-an eventually produced a couple of lines. Guei-lung didn't say anything, although he rolled his eyes.

Their game went on for another hour, but Mei-hua knew she had already won. Guei-lung stopped baiting her with words loaded with double meanings. Throughout the game, he peeked over at her, as if trying to figure something out, but not quite able to do it.

CHAPTER 11

SEVERAL WEEKS WENT BY with Mei-hua silently serving Ping-an. She found her job wasn't difficult. As Orchid had told her, she didn't need to do any heavy housework; she wasn't even required to clean up Ping-an's messes. No, Madam Wu had wanted a companion for her daughter, someone her age. Therefore, although Mei-hua couldn't speak, she easily fulfilled these simple tasks, since simply being with Ping-an and listening to her chatter on about her clothing, her hair, or the parties she attended, was enough.

One cool morning, Mei-hua and Ping-an sat in the garden by the fish pond when Guei-lung came along. "Ping-an, play chess with me. I'm bored," he said.

"Wait a minute. Come see the new fish Auntie Lao put in our pond."

Guei-lung came up to the little bridge and stood

next to her. Mei-hua moved away from Ping-an, going to sit under a nearby willow. The sun filtered through the tree's branches, its warmth penetrating the light blue jacket of the new clothes Madam Wu had made for her.

"How can you stand her?" Guei-lung asked, jerking his head toward Mei-hua.

"I like her. She's easy to have around."

"Anyone would be better than her. She can't talk; she's cursed."

"I don't believe that. And, anyway, so what? I don't care if she can't talk. She does whatever I tell her to do, and never snitches on me to Mom. Plus, she never complains and never tries to wheedle extra favors or treats the way the other maids do."

"Why are you always complaining about her, Guei-lung? She's not your maid; she's mine."

"She doesn't act like a servant," Guei-lung returned.

"What do you mean, 'doesn't act like a servant'?" his sister laughed. "I just told you she does whatever I want her to do, and she never complains. What more do you want?"

"Look at her: how she walks, how she sits, how she stands. Too much pride in every move. You'd think she's the mistress."

"Why, Guei-lung, I didn't know you paid such close attention to my maids!" his sister said in mock surprise.

Guei-lung snapped back, "Don't you notice anything! She's not like the others."

Ping-an glanced over at Mei-hua. "Yes, you're right, older brother. Look at her now. From the way she's holding her head, I'd guess she's a princess." His sister giggled.

"Okay, make fun of me. But, there's something

different about that one." Then he waved a hand in dismissal and changed the subject. "How about a game of chess? You need to practice before your teacher gets here."

Ping-an made a face. The teacher. How she hated him. She never knew her characters and he never tired of scolding her. Although her parents realized she was not exceptionally bright, they wanted her to know enough to please an educated husband. And since her father loved chess, they insisted the tutor also teach their daughter the game in addition to reading and writing. Unfortunately for Ping-an, she didn't like learning chess any more than studying her characters.

Before Ping-an could think of another excuse to get out of playing the dreaded game with her brother, Orchid brought news of Ping-an's teacher's arrival. Moping, Ping-an called to Mei-hua and told her they had to leave. The two entered an adjoining room where Teacher Song, a stern and colorless man, waited.

Mei-hua kept an impassive face, but her heart rejoiced. As an ignorant bondservant, no one expected her to be educated. Only wealthy families could afford private tutors. Wherever towns set up public schools for the lower classes, they were for boys only. People believed only boys needed to be literate, and even they generally required no more than basic knowledge—just enough arithmetic and reading ability to know if they were being cheated when buying and selling. Educating poor girls was considered a waste of time and money.

Teacher Song lacked vitality in his teaching, but at least his being there provided a change of pace. Most of her time with Ping-an was boring; each day dragged into the next with a crushing sameness. Ping-an's idea of a perfect day consisted of doing no more than to sit and embroider or dress up and go visiting. Unfortunately for Mei-hua, as Ping-an's companion, she was expected to sew and visit as well. And while skilled in calligraphy, reading, and composing songs and poems, she was miserable at sewing and other domestic tasks.

"Ping-an, did you bring the characters you were supposed to work on since our last class?" Teacher Song greeted her.

Ping-an's hand flew to her mouth. "Oh, Sir, I forgot." Turning to leave, she added, "I'll go get them immediately."

"Sit down, Ping-an; Mei-hua will fetch them." Turning toward Mei-hua he said, "You do know where her papers are, don't you?"

Mei-hua nodded her head and instantly disappeared out the door. She fairly skipped along the veranda. Entering Ping-an's room, a teak box caught her eye. It sat on a long narrow table pushed against the far wall. Without breaking her stride, she went straight to the box and removed its intricately carved lid.

"What are you doing?" a masculine voice demanded.

Startled, she spun around and found herself staring into Guei-lung's righteous eyes.

Quickly pulling out a rolled sheet of cream colored paper, she replaced the lid, and—with a show of humility—extended Ping-an's clumsy writings toward him.

"Oh, I see." He almost sounded sorry for the accusation in his voice. Taking the paper, he looked at it. "If she were a chicken, I'd say she had real style."

Mei-hua almost laughed. His sister's penmanship had to be the worst she had ever seen. The page full of characters resembled random scratches more than actual words.

Seeing the touch of a smile on her lips at his comments, Guei-lung suddenly pushed the long paper back at Mei-hua. "You'd better take these. Her teacher must be waiting," he said gruffly.

Mei-hua felt her face flush. What had she done wrong? He was the one who made a joke at his sister's expense. No matter what Mei-hua did, it was never right where Guei-lung was concerned.

Carefully rerolling the rice paper, she bowed to the young master and, with as much deference as possible, took her leave. She may not have heavy housework to do, but she was beginning to understand that being a servant wasn't easy—especially when it came to pleasing the family.

I never realized servants had to be so diplomatic just to get through a day, she thought as she walked back to the classroom.

Upon her return, Mei-hua gave the assignment paper to Ping-an, who in turn handed it to her teacher.

"What is this? What kind of writing is this?" Teacher Song cried when he took the papers from Mei-hua and cast a brief glimpse over Ping-an's assignment. "Haven't you learned anything? No one can write this badly! You're not trying! You're a disgrace to your parents." He started scolding long and loud. An avalanche of ferocious and cruel words spewed out and out and out. Ping-an sat, head down, speechless. Unheeded, tears rolled over her pale cheeks.

Mei-hua had heard him dump his anger and frustrations on Ping-an before. She felt sorry for the rich girl. No one expected much of her, but she didn't seem to be able to accomplish even the simple assignments.

After screaming at Ping-an until he was almost hoarse, Teacher Song gave her another writing assignment. Handing her a copy of a Confucian Classic written in a beautiful style, he said, "Follow the strokes exactly. Even you cannot go wrong if you follow this example."

Ping-an dutifully worked on her new assignment, tears still lining her dark eyelashes. Teacher Song sat at a nearby table with his back to her, reading. During this time, no one expected Mei-hua to do anything except sit and wait. The idea of including her in the lessons verged on the ridiculous. When the young mistress could not do the work, how could a mute indentured servant, a mere maid, be expected to do it?

There were times when Mei-hua went numb with boredom. It was bad enough she had to sit there like a dummy day after day, week after week, but there were so many books in the room, right within reach. If only she could open one up and lose herself in its words.

She desperately wanted something to do. If only she could complete Ping-an's work for her! The part of the school day Mei-hua liked most was when Teacher Song lectured on the Confucian Classics or about Chinese history. In time, he started expanding his daily lecturing, because—in spite of her attempts to remain uninvolved in the classroom—he noticed her interest in these subjects. She tried to appear disinterested, hiding her enthusiasm and pleasure, but there were times when he seemed to lecture directly to her instead of to Ping-an.

Fortunately, Ping-an didn't mind. She liked it. She hated being the only student, the sole object of her teacher's unrelenting irritation. The more attention he paid to her maid, the less she had to do herself. Now as he lectured more often and longer than usual, Ping-an developed what she hoped appeared to be an attentive gaze, behind which she could daydream until he finished speaking.

But today, Teacher Song's ire never let up. Ping-an wasn't progressing and, if she failed to improve, her parents would surely blame him. They'd fire him and he would be out of work. All because of his pupil's stupidity.

Today he didn't bother with a lecture; he gave his hapless student one copying assignment after another. He tried, briefly, to hear a memorization lesson he had given her, but she could only stumble through its beginning. Scowling, he ordered her to finish memorizing it and, at the same time, gave her several new pages to learn.

It was a tough day for Ping-an. Mei-hua regarded her mistress with sympathy. Many years ago she had to learn these same assignments. What Ping-an found insurmountable, however, she had found to be easy and fun. If only she could help this unhappy student!

Finally, the hours of tutoring were almost over. "Bring your completed papers to me!" Teacher Song demanded as he impatiently rose to take them off her writing table.

Ping-an promptly began assembling the papers scattered around her, but he didn't wait for her to finish. He thrust his hand out to grab them off her table. As he reached forward and his hand dropped on Ping-an's written assignments, his long gray sleeve swept over her inkstone. It landed unceremoniously in the pool of lush black liquid. Instantly realizing what had happened, he pulled back, causing his ink soaked sleeve to toss drops of black over the table, papers, and front of his clothing.

"Oh, my robe!" he cried. He grabbed at the ink-laden sleeve with his left hand, but the cloth swung away from him, as if with a life of its own. He frantically lifted his sleeve and again sought to gather it up. This only succeeded in getting more ink on his clothing as again jet black droplets cascaded onto his long gown.

Sputtering and fuming at the inky mess, he managed a tight lipped, "You are dismissed!" and stormed from the room.

The girls stared at each other in shock and then began a rolling, silent giggle. He had looked so funny.

"Oh, we shouldn't laugh," Ping-an said and giggled again. "He might come back." She leaned sideways to peer out the window. She wanted to catch a glimpse of Teacher Song to make sure he was leaving.

Still grinning and nodding her head, Mei-hua began cleaning the inky mess. Yet, as she quickly and efficiently put things in order, she noticed Ping-an remained quiet. They finally left the small classroom, and Ping-an made her way back to her rooms even more slowly than usual.

When they arrived, Ping-an crossed over to a chair. Sitting with a sigh, she said, "All my parents want me to do is learn to read that book on being a good daughter, daughter-in-law, and wife. Then they could tell my future parents-in-law that I am educated." Her voice was soft and low.

Her young mistress was more depressed over this day's classroom disasters than Mei-hua had ever seen her. She glanced at the scroll with the modest young woman humbly serving her elders. It seemed to contrast with Ping-an's writing table, which overflowed with ornaments and clothing accessories.

After a pensive moment, Ping-an turned to Mei-hua, "I would like some tea and a small snack of sweet rice dumplings. Go to the kitchen and get it for me."

Mei-hua nodded and strolled off toward the kitchen in the further courtyard. Delighted at the order, a song of joy played in her head. She had not been out of the women's courtyard for more than a week. This small outing provided an opportunity for gathering gossip from the other servants. As she had expected when she first entered the house and discovered Ping'an's age, being her personal maid was quite restrictive. If Mei-hua remained stuck away, how was she ever going to discover more about the official Hangzhou families and find her father's friend?

Approaching the back of the compound and the kitchen, she could hear only the rhythmic chopping sound of the cook preparing for dinner. Sure enough, when she peeked into the room, it was empty except for the sturdy cook standing over a well-worn wooden table. Never going out much herself, the cook had no gossip from any other household besides this one. However, that did not keep her from talking incessantly to anyone who came into her domain. Mei-hua's muteness gave the cook no pause as she chatted about everything from the quality of the chickens found in the market this morning to the amount of rice left and the need to purchase more. Although none of this information was useful to Mei-hua, she nevertheless enjoyed the break from her normal duties and lingered in the kitchen to listen to the friendly cook's prattling about this and that.

However, eventually Mei-hua realized she'd been gone far longer than she intended. Ping-an might be upset at such an extended absence. Given today's difficulties for her mistress, Mei-hua didn't want to cause more problems. She hurried back to Ping-an as fast as the full tea pot and tray of goodies allowed.

Putting on a pleasant face to cheer Ping-an, Mei-hua walked through the open door, expecting to see her young mistress sitting with her cosmetics containers. Whenever she was upset, Ping-an took up the small jars and brushes and practiced putting on make-up. But to Mei-hua's surprise, the girl wasn't in her chamber. After a quick glance around, Mei-hua realized none of the other maids were around either. An ominous sensation filled the otherwise empty room.

Just as Mei-hua turned to leave, she noticed a sheet of practice paper left among Ping-an's cosmetics. With a sense of dread, she went over, picked it up, and read:

Honorable Parents,

I am a disgrace to my family. I can learn nothing and I can do nothing.

My body will be in the garden well. Even though I am a disgrace, please take it out and bury it so that my spirit will not haunt our home.

Your humble daughter,
Ping-an

The note was simple, yet practical. Even as she planned to commit suicide, Ping-an worried about her family. Not only was suicide considered a child's most grievous sign of disrespect to her family—because she willingly destroyed the body her family had given her—it was common knowledge that a drowned person's spirit could harm anyone who came near the place they died. The only antidote was to remove the victim's body from its watery grave and give it a proper burial.

Panic gripped Mei-hua. She grabbed the note and dashed to the garden. Ping-an's embroidered, silk-lined, outer coat lay crumpled on the ground next to the well.

Mei-hua immediately turned back toward the garden gate. There was no way she could get Ping-an out of the well by herself.

A house full of people and no one around during an emergency. Her heart raced. Its rapid thumping was all she could hear. She had to find someone to help. But, who?

CHAPTER 12

JUST THEN, Mei-hua heard Guei-lung's voice coming from his room on the other side of a short garden wall, saying his lessons out loud. She ran to his door and threw it open.

"What the...!"

Mei-hua, panting hard, grabbed his hand and started pulling him toward the door. Although she was obviously desperate, Guei-lung and his private tutor had no idea what was causing such alarm. Still pulling on Guei-lung's arm, she handed Ping-an's note to the teacher. With a glance at the paper, he cried, "Aiya! Your sister is trying to drown herself in the garden well. We must find her!"

They burst out of the room and sprinted to the courtyard. At the sight of his sister's coat lying near the well, he ran to it and called down into the deep hole, "Little Sister! I'm here! Hold onto the rock wall; I'm coming for you!"

A faint mumble answered his call. The three nodded grimly to each other. At least Ping-an was still alive.

Guei-lung jumped onto the well's bucket and, grabbing its rope, told his teacher and Mei-hua to lower him down into the well. Hearing the commotion, a husky fellow covered in dust and mud rushed into the garden. A mason, he had been repairing a small building in the back garden.

The teacher called to him and said, "Take the crank from the girl."

Even though Mei-hua gripped the handle until her knuckles were white, Guei-lung's weight on the line threatened to yank the crank out of her hands. If that happened, he could fall into the well and knock his sister completely under water. The mason's massive hand closed over the handle allowing Mei-hua to step back while he assisted the teacher in slowly lowering Guei-lung into the well.

Once down, Guei-lung called, "Stop!"

They stood in silence, peering into the hole, seeing nothing but darkness. Muted sounds of movement gave them little indication of what was happening below.

Mei-hua leaned over the well's wall, straining to see into the darkness. Nothing. The minutes dragged by, a seeming eternity. She pressed her forehead against her hand, willing Guei-lung and Ping-an to safety.

"Okay, pull us up!" Guei-lung's voice finally sounded from the hallow depths. Mei-hua jumped back. The two men grabbed onto the handle and, with a steady, slow pace, started pulling the bucket up. As the top of two heads appeared, the teacher steadied the bucket until it was even with the top of the well. Guei-lung handed his water-soaked treasure over to the mason, who gently took the limp body in his massive arms. Guei-lung then quickly jumped out and bent over gasping for breath. Even as he sucked in air, he never took his eyes off his sister. She lay cradled in the mason's arms, ghostly pale, eyes closed, and barely breathing.

By this time, a crowd had gathered around, their father Hsu Dou-wu and their mother among them.

"Move aside!" Hsu Dou-wu ordered. After reviewing the scene for a moment, he told the mason, "Carry her to her bed."

Then, "Orchid, Lily, attend to her!"

He spun around to another servant. "Get a doctor. When he arrives, bring him to her room immediately!"

More commotion followed. Mei-hua, along with the other servants, ran here and there getting water, hot tea, clean clothing, and blankets. Within a short time, an itinerant doctor appeared in the doorway, halting everyone's frantic movements. Servants and family alike waited in silence, listening, anxiously straining to catch the doctor's comments on how she was doing and if she would be all right.

After a while, Master Hsu's imposing figure appeared in the doorway. Without a word he briskly strode down the veranda. Madam Wu emerged from her daughter's room next and, after a brief glance around, said, "Ping-an's all right. Go back to your work."

She turned away, but before returning, she looked long and sadly at Mei-hua. "Go to the kitchen and help the cook. I'll call you when you're needed." With that, she reentered her daughter's room.

Puzzled, Mei-hua wondered why she was being sent

away. Clearly, her young mistress needed her. She started for the kitchen, her heart heavy with questions and concern.

Rapid footsteps on the wooden walkway brought her to attention. Guei-lung hurried into the courtyard and walked directly toward her. Stepping near, he caught her glance and held it. After a moment, he quietly said, "Thanks. Thank you for saving Ping-an's life." With a nod towards the courtyard's gate, he added, "Father wants to see you right away. In the library. Follow me."

Walking behind Guei-lung, she noticed how straight and tall he stood as he stepped along with an easy, steady gait. Without bound feet, Mei-hua had no trouble keeping up.

He stopped at the library door and whirled around, as if expecting to have to wait for her. His quick and unexpected stop caused Mei-hua to collide into him. He grabbed her and held her near him to steady them and keep them from tumbling over each other. She couldn't breathe.

"Ah, excuse me, Mei-hua," he finally said in a whisper, as if embarrassed. He didn't release her or move back.

Once again, muteness saved her. His nearness, his embrace stole her voice—she couldn't have spoken if she wanted to. She wondered if he felt her heart. Never had it beat this hard and this loud!

"Guei-lung? Are you there?" an authoritative voice rumbled through the closed doorway.

He quickly released her and called into the room. "Yes, I'm here. I have Ping-an's maid with me." Awkwardly, he added to Mei-hua, "Come along; he's waiting."

They walked single file into the library with Guei-lung in the lead. Guei-lung moved to his father's side and she stopped in the middle of the room, facing Master Hsu.

She bowed her head but her quick eyes still managed to take in every detail. Ping-an's father sat behind a heavy, dark table with writing implements and blank paper on one side and a pile of official looking documents on the other. In the center of the table, Mei-hua recognized Ping-an's crumbled note telling of her intention to commit suicide.

"Mei-hua," Master Hsu began, "my son tells me you brought this note to him. Is that true?"

Mei-hua nodded. Nervous, she wondered why he asked.

"Did you know Ping-an wanted to kill herself?" The last two words came out low and softly as if he had a hard time even saying them.

Mei-hua violently shook her head, "no."

"Were you with her when she wrote this note?"

Again Mei-hua shook her head.

"You're her personal maid," he thundered. "Where were you?"

Ah, now she understood. *He blames me*, she thought, *for not being with Ping-an and keeping her from trying to commit suicide.* She understood his anger, but she also knew it was misplaced. She needed to tell him Ping-an had sent her away on an errand, but how was she to do this without a voice?

Guei-lung broke into the conversation. "Father, she's not to blame." He cast a steady gaze at her. "Perhaps Ping-an sent her away."

Before he could suggest more alternatives, Mei-hua pointed at him and vigorously nodded her head.

"She had sent you away," his father repeated, but his

stare said he didn't fully believe her.

Mei-hua nodded again, then fell to her knees, arms spread out in front of her in abject apology. For although she hadn't known what Ping-an was planning, she knew, as her maid, she would be held accountable for her mistress's behavior.

"Never mind." A reasonable man, Master Hsu appeared ready to consider this young servant's innocence in his daughter's near tragedy. Still, something here bothered him. He looked down at the paper with its poorly formed characters and then at the bondmaid.

"You knew what this note said, didn't you?" he asked, his voice non-threatening, inviting her to be honest.

A tremor ran through her. She remained silently kneeling with her head down, face toward the floor. She had given herself away.

The only way she could have known what the note said was if Ping-an had told her, or if she had read it herself. Since he no longer appeared to believe the former, he must realize she could read. After her hasty actions, she had hoped that her part in this rescue drama would go unnoticed. After all, she rationalized, she was just a simple bondservant and—like most servants—all but invisible to others. But this was not to be today.

"Look up," he ordered.

Mei-hua lifted her head and fixed her eyes on his chest.

You read the note before giving it to my son," he continued. "That's how you knew what she planned to do and where to find her."

Guei-lung jerked his head up and stared at Mei-hua.

She blinked and dropped her eyes, fearing they would betray too much of her secret. Slowly, she nodded.

"Rise and come closer to the table," he said.

Mei-hua walked to the table, her head filled with questions about what would happen now. Certainly he wouldn't punish her, she hoped, because she didn't do anything wrong. They never asked her about her education—or lack of it—so she hadn't lied to them. Lying would have been a serious offense, one demanding dismissal.

"Can you also write?"

Startled, she paused. If she admitted to being able to write, they could find out all kinds of information about her background, her family. She could lie to him and take the chance. How would they discover what she knew if she didn't admit to being literate?

She carefully studied Master Hsu's face for a second before answering. He had the same kindly eyes as her father. He seemed to honestly want her to trust him and—perhaps—he was trustworthy, just like her father. She found herself wanting to believe it, to believe in him.

She nodded.

Putting the note aside, he took a piece of blank paper and placed it in the center of his desk. He filled a brush with ink and handed it to Mei-hua.

"Write your name," he ordered.

A simple request.

Her heart turned cold; her hand trembled. She took the brush and, pushing back her fears, quickly wrote "Mei-hua" in the center of the paper.

Master Hsu smiled slightly as he watched her write. Who would have expected such strong, finely shaped characters from a servant and a simple girl at that? Well-formed writing signaled an intelligent mind and a good teacher. A look of surprise and delight at finding such a treasure in their daughter's new maid momentarily lit his eyes.

"That's fine," he said. His voice remained neutral, controlled. "I understand Mei-hua is the name we call you, but what was your name before you came to this house?"

This was the request Mei-hua dreaded most. She must never divulge her family name; doing so would cause harm to herself and, more importantly, to her father and her family, wherever they were. Her hands began to sweat. What should she do? She felt a warmth emanating from her jade and knew she needed to be careful.

Just then, a loud banging was heard from the hallway. Mei-hua started. Were these the soldiers that had come to her father's office the last night she was there? Had they found her here in this house, even disguised as a bondservant? It didn't make sense, but her pulse raced with the certainty of it.

"Enter!" Master Hsu commanded.

A robust, muscular man wearing a dark robe with broad, sweeping sleeves immediately marched into the center of the room. With a sharp forward thrust of his head and shoulders, he bowed and announced, "Sir! I have an order from the Emperor!"

Master Hsu turned to Guei-lung. "Take this maid back to your sister's quarters. I will continue our meeting later."

Mei-hua hardly heard his commands. Her chest constricted and her breathing came hard. The Emperor! Master Hsu works for the Emperor! She was in the house of the enemy!

CHAPTER 13

WITHOUT A WORD, Guei-lung indicated she should follow him. Mei-hua bowed and walked backwards as she made her way out of the library as fast as possible. Fortunately for her, Master Hsu's attention was now completely captured by the newly arrived problem. He and the messenger spoke to each other in rapid, quiet voices too low for her to understand.

Her heart beat a funeral dirge as she followed Guei-lung. They passed along the Master's veranda and through an arched gateway into the next garden.

An official! She couldn't believe her bad luck. What were the odds of ending up here, in his house, as his bondservant? Did he know about her father? What would he do if he discovered Magistrate Zhang Xue-wen's daughter lived in his house? And he would, she thought gloomily. She was sure of it.

She was sure little got past him once he took an

interest. Up to this point, she had merely been an extension of the women's world in his household, so he didn't interfere. However, his daughter's near death cast an unwavering light on her and her mismatched identity. A mute bondservant was strange. A literate, mute, bondservant was unheard of. The incongruity of it all must surely intrigue him, as it would anyone. He would search out whatever he could discover about her and her background. His curiosity alone demanded it.

I only have one choice now, Mei-hua thought. *I must escape.* She reasoned they wouldn't put as much effort in hunting for an escaped servant as they would for the daughter of a suspected traitor—a magistrate, a government official wanted by the Emperor for treason.

Walking behind Guei-lung, lost in thought, she once again bumped into him when he stopped just inside the garden gate. He laughed lightly.

"Do you make it a habit to walk into people?" he grinned.

Flustered, Mei-hua quickly bowed deeply to him.

"You don't need to apologize. I was just joking." Then, after pausing a moment, he asked, "How is it you're literate? Even my sister, who has a good teacher, has trouble learning to read and write. Who taught you? Where did you study? What books did you learn?"

Guei-lung was not Master Hsu and Mei-hua neither feared him nor stood in awe of him. His questions weren't guided by years of experience in interrogating people, as his father's had been. They came out of interest and simple fascination.

Mei-hu merely smiled slightly and gave him another, more playful bow as if to say, "How can I answer you, when I cannot speak?"

"Right! You're right! No problem. Later you can

write out your answers. Now, you must return to Ping-an's quarters, as Father ordered."

Just then, his mother appeared at Ping-an's door. Leaning more heavily than usual on the two maids assisting her, worry etched on her drawn face, she saw Mei-hua and she stiffened.

"What are you doing here wasting time talking?" she demanded. "I told you to go down to the kitchen!"

"Mother, Father told her to return to Ping'an's room," Guei-lung quickly interjected in a soothing, even tone.

"Your father? When did he say that?"

"A moment ago. He had Mei-hua come to his study to answer a few questions, but a messenger interrupted with important business. So, he told me to bring her back here."

"All right. I'm glad he was interrogating her," she said looking closely at Ping'an's maid.

Mei-hua felt struck by the word "interrogating," as if she were a criminal. What did Madam Wu mean? Did she also think Mei-hua had aided her daughter's suicide attempt and blamed her for it?

Furrowing her brow and shaking her head, Madam Wu added, "I feel there is something wrong here and she's a part of it."

"Mama, I'm sure she didn't do anything wrong. Ping-an is alive right now because of her quick action in getting Teacher Gao and me. We should thank her, not punish her," Guei-lung spoke persuasively.

"Perhaps. We'll see," she said, still sounding unconvinced. "The doctor said someone probably enticed her to try to...harm herself. I don't think she would've done such a thing on her own."

Mei-hua, alarmed at Madam Wu's suspicions,

clasped her hands to her chest and vigorously shook her head at these words.

At this silent plea, Madam Wu appeared to soften. "Well, we'll see. We'll see. I'm aware Ping-an has grown fond of this girl. Nevertheless, you must realize how serious this situation is, Guei-lung."

"Yes, Mama, I know."

"Mei-hua," Madam Wu continued, "you may go into Ping'an's room as Master Hsu ordered. However, Orchid will be taking care of my daughter. You will take your orders from Orchid. Remain there until Master Hsu is able to complete his questioning." She turned to go, a maid on either side of her. Resting a hand on each of them, she paused momentarily.

"Guei-lung," she said over her shoulder, "return to your studies. You don't need to spend time here. The doctor is taking care of your sister. There is nothing for you to do."

With that, Madam Wu leaned into the support her maids provided and glided down the veranda and through the garden gate, her tiny golden lotus feet skimming along the walkway. As with her daughter, it was impossible for her to walk without her servants' assistance.

Smiling, Guei-lung wrapped his left hand over his right and, holding them chest height, gave Mei-hua a silent "good luck" by rocking them back and forth in her direction. Mei-hua gracefully bowed a "thank you" back to him before they turned away from each other.

Through this exchange, Mei-hua managed to keep a calm face, but troubling thoughts raced around her mind. The Master was about to discover her identity, and the Mistress believed she had caused her daughter's near tragedy. She had to escape before either took definite steps against her. There was no choice; she had to develop a plan. And soon.

CHAPTER 14

ORCHID PERCHED ON A SMALL STOOL near their young mistress's kang; a couple of other maids quietly sat across the room from them. Seeing Mei-hua, Orchid smiled a welcome and silently held her hand up, telling her to stop where she was. Without a sound, Orchid rose and came to stand next to her so they could talk without bothering the young mistress.

"I'm glad you're back." She whispered in a barely audible voice. "I'm sure Young Mistress doesn't blame you for what happened, and she'll be happy to have you here."

Her voice was infused with a mix of concern and kindness, but her words shot straight to Mei-hua's heart. *Blame you.* It seems Orchid had already heard the theory that Mei-hua was somehow responsible for Ping-an's suicide attempt!

"Stay with the others," Orchid said, and waved a

hand toward the two maids. "If anything is needed, I'll call you."

Sitting with Ping-an's personal maids, Mei-hua tried to work out a plan. She hadn't done very well so far. She knew nothing of her father's friend, and her own situation had gotten worse. She was fully aware that knowing she had to escape and actually escaping were two different things.

Getting out of such a large, well organized household was as difficult as breaking into it. Even a tall, athletic man could not scale the soaring walls encircling the compound, and guards stood at the ready at each of the gates leading to the outside. Simply walking out of here would never work. She would be stopped and questioned. After all, personal maids never went out alone on errands. For one, they might flee their masters—her plan exactly—and for another, they might be attacked by dangerous strangers. A quagmire of complications and problems uneasily shifted around her thoughts. Just as she was about to give up, an insight flashed through the morass. She grinned; she knew what to do.

Finally, the light filtering through the paper-covered windows became dim. Orchid told Mei-hua to light three round lanterns. One had the word *ping* written on each side; the other two had images of young women painted on them. The lanterns' flickering light spilled out, filling the room with a soft glow. The cook's helper brought dinner to the room for them all, placing the tray of dishes on a low rectangular table in the center of the room.

"Your dinner is here, mistress," Orchid said, her voice kind and encouraging.

Ping-an did not stir. The doctor's medications had

put her into a deep sleep, and that's where she remained.

Madam Wu came by to check on her daughter and to oversee Orchid and Ping-an's maids. She told them to go to bed one at a time. The others were to remain sitting and attentive, watching over Ping-an, alert for any change.

Mei-hua insisted she be the last to go rest. By the time her turn came, however, all of the maids, including Orchid, had fallen asleep with their heads resting on their arms on the table or slumped back against the wall. Only a couple more hours of night remained. Soon the cook would be in the kitchen preparing breakfast for the household.

As Mei-hua left Ping-an, she turned down the veranda toward the maids' quarters. However, as she walked into the inky black shadow of a large overhanging willow tree, she turned sharply and silently crossed the gardens to the still-empty kitchen.

She stopped just inside the doorway of the darkened room, letting her eyes adjust to the dim interior. Slowly, she began to make out rounded silhouettes of varying heights and sizes. Storage jars and pans rested around the floor and on the stoves' surfaces.

Groping along the wall to the left, her hand touched something soft and pliable. Just where she had hoped it would be! The cook had left her protective outer robe hanging on a post, ready for her when she came in the morning. The pungent odor of oil, spices, and garlic permeated the rough cloth. A smile played across Mei-hua's lips; finally, things were going her way.

She removed the robe from its wooden peg, slipped out of her own fine silk outer layer, and wrapped herself in the cook's smelly garment. Without pausing, she tied the front closed and again felt along the wall, reaching for a shoulder pole and the baskets which normally swung at each end. The cook had stacked the pole and baskets together near several sacks of rice. Mei-hua grabbed them and, since the baskets had covers, she didn't stop to take anything else to put into them. She hated taking more than needed for her subterfuge.

Satisfied, she stepped out of the kitchen and slipped a basket on either end of the pole before hoisting it onto her shoulder. Even though the baskets were empty, she found it difficult to control their movement at first. The unaccustomed load pressed into her flesh as she started toward the back gate leading to the outside world. A sense of relief surged through her as every step brought her closer to freedom.

She had almost reached the door leading to the street when a voice from the shadows asked, "Where are you going in such a hurry and so early in the morning, Mei-hua?"

CHAPTER 15

MEI-HUA STARTED at the sound of the voice, nearly dropping her baskets and pole. *Remember, be silent*, she told herself as she faced the unseen speaker.

"What are you up to?" the voice asked again.

Guei-lung stepped out of the shadows. A frown marred his handsome face. "Why are you dressed like the cook?" He waved an impatient hand up and down indicating her rough clothing.

Mei-hua let the pole slip off her shoulders. Oh,no! Now it would be harder than ever to try to escape! Once caught, they will watch her more closely than ever.

"It looks like you're trying to leave. Why? What's wrong?" His questions kept coming.

Silent, Mei-hua stood with shoulders slumped and head down as she cursed her luck.

Stepping close to her, Guei-lung put a hand on her arm. "Mei-hua, I understand. You're afraid my parents will punish you for Ping-an's near tragedy." His face showed concern. "Don't be." He straightened his shoulders and stood straighter. "I'll make sure you're okay. After all, if it weren't for you, my sister wouldn't be with us now. I know Father realizes this; Mother will soon."

The sincerity in his voice touched Mei-hua. She believed he would try to protect her, but he had no idea of the threat hounding her. The danger she faced dwarfed anything he could possibly help her with. Plus, she knew if he assisted her in any way he would be putting his own family in terrible jeopardy. If the Emperor did indict her father with crimes against the state, Guei-lung and his family would then be involved too. By association alone, they would be pulled into the treacherous legal system, where everyone is guilty until proven innocent.

"Come. Let's go back before anyone misses you and you really do get in trouble!" he said, trying to be cheerful.

He picked up the pole and baskets and guided her back into the kitchen, where she removed the coarse, soiled kitchen jacket and put on her own silken wrap.

"That's better," Guei-lung grinned as he inhaled the jacket's delicate scent. "The smell of garlic will never win out over jasmine's fragrance." Mei-hua felt his breath on the back of her neck and shivered despite its warmth.

Composing herself, she stepped away and nodded with a small smile. She must be agreeable until she had time to work out another plan.

Steering her back through the gardens, Guei-lung chatted quietly into her ear. "Bet you wonder how I happened to see you leaving, huh?"

She nodded.

"Well, when I can't sleep, like tonight, I walk through the deserted courtyards. Usually deserted, that is. This time, however, I spotted a figure slipping into the herb garden and then into the kitchen. I knew it was you."

She stopped short and gave him an inquiring look.

"It's your walk," he answered with a smug grin, "I'd know it anywhere. Not that it's clumsy," he hastened to add, thinking back to when he had laughed at her big feet. "It's stately, dignified. Not like any of the other servants. But not like any of the women in my family either. Your step isn't mincing, like my mother and sister's, but it's elegant nonetheless."

She knew he was trying to flatter her this time, but his attempts to explain her walk made her silently laugh. At first he was taken aback by her reaction, but then he laughed, too. His laughter rang out over the courtyard.

"And, you know, you'll never fool anyone into believing you're a cook or a vegetable seller, even with a pole and baskets. Your walk will always give you away."

Guei-lung paused with Mei-hua as they were about to pass under the doorway between the herb garden and the courtyard in front of the maids' rooms.

"I won't go with you to the maids' quarters. Mother wouldn't like it." He stood back and pushed the hair out of his eyes. Her heart caught at the concern and care they revealed as he stared down at her. "Remember this: you don't have to worry. Everything will be all right. I promise you."

Mei-hua wished the world was that simple; everything seemed so impossible. Still, she nodded.

He gently touched her sleeve. "See you later," he

said. Then he was gone, engulfed by the shadows.

Over the next several days, Ping-an improved markedly. She remained under the care of an itinerant doctor, a man who had learned his medical skills through an apprenticeship. He practiced his trade daily in the neighborhoods surrounding the compound. People called him a bell doctor because he let them know his services were available by ringing a bell as he walked through the streets. Now he came several times a day to attend to Ping-an. Such care was expensive, but the cost was meaningless; her health was what mattered to her family.

After plying the young girl with strong herbs to make her rest, the bell doctor announced that no human had forced her to attempt suicide; a water spirit living at the bottom of the well caused her to jump into it. Immediately after this pronouncement, Ping-an's mother hired a medium to drive the water spirit out.

A nervous excitement hung in the air throughout the rest of the day as the servants prepared for the evening's exorcism. While the sounds of stringed instruments and drums signaling special divination or exorcism rituals could be heard on many a night throughout the city, this would be the first for the Hsu household.

"What if the spirit doesn't leave?" Orchid asked, hand over her mouth as if to mute the question in case the spirit could hear her. "Will it be angry at us for trying to get rid of it and force more people into the well?"

The maids sat in a corner of Ping-an's room, heads together in quiet conversation. Orchid's question disturbed them all. If the spirit made Ping-an jump into the well, it could cause any one of them to do the same.

If they did, would someone come to save them in time? They cast nervous glances at their young mistress recovering now with the help of the itinerant doctor's medicines.

"Don't talk like that," one of the maids mumbled in a low voice. The others nodded. They knew that what people said could easily become a reality. It was best to avoid harmful energy by never mentioning it.

Orchid ducked her head. They were right. She fell silent.

Mei-hua wanted to tell them not to worry, but even she wondered what had pushed Ping-an to the point of trying to commit suicide. Was it a water spirit? Or was it her sense of being a complete failure? Could such feelings really cause her to jump into the well? Mei-hua wished her father were here and she could discuss the question with him. But he wasn't and she had no one else to turn to; she had to work out these concerns on her own.

The household remained in suspended animation throughout the day and into the evening. No one spoke above a murmur and the servants seemed to carry out their duties on noiseless feet. As the soothing darkness filled every crevice, they heard the growing rhythmic sound of clanging and strumming.

Mei-hua and the other maids rushed to the courtyard to see what was happening. They stayed in the shadows where they could see but not be seen.

Soon the compound's front gates opened to admit a parade. It was led by a man wearing long, loose white pants and a billowing white jacket tied around his waist by a red cord. He carried a triangular flag displaying a mystical character embroidered on it in bright, primary colors. Coming up immediately behind him was a troupe of musicians, a small group of men wearing identical outfits in white with a red sash tied around their jackets. Lastly, one fellow carrying another triangular flag held up the procession's rear. As doors and gates opened before them, they marched through the public courtyard and into the magistrate family's private garden.

Mei-hua noticed that a ritual table had been set up near the well. An assistant had placed paper strips, ink, an inkstone, a brush, and a plain, round incense bowl on top of its smooth surface.

The music stopped and in silence the men in white continued forward, approaching the raised table. They divided into two rows and lined up on either side of it. One man, the medium, strode forward. He held three incense sticks representing Heaven, Earth, and Humankind in front of him at chest level. He dropped to his knees, raising the incense high above his head; the other men also fell to their knees. Then, standing again, the medium thrust the incense into the bowl's sand. An assistant lit them as he stood before the altar and prayed. As a medium, he was asking another—helpful—other-worldly spirit to use his body as a vessel. He wanted the spirit to come and help fight against the evil spirit in the well. Mei-hua breathed in the delicate fragrance of unfamiliar herbs as they wafted through the air.

The clanging music started up again and several of the men began a loud, throaty intonation. Their ritual chanting invited the medium's spirit to enter his body. Soon he started rapidly walking in a circle between his two lines of assistants. Periodically, he would stop and begin shaking uncontrollably; then he would walk in a circle again, stop, and begin shaking once more. All the while, his movements became more and more violent. One man jumped forward, grabbing the medium as he leapt into the air; another joined the first, clutching at the flailing body to keep him from falling as a powerful spirit took hold. The spirit had arrived to do battle with the water spirit.

Once the frenzied trembling quieted down and the medium stood quietly alert, his assistants hurriedly dressed him in a new skirt and jacket of brilliant red. Emblazoned on the jacket were embroidered symbols of power and harmony: a swirling golden dragon on its back and an imposing black-and-white divided circle on its front.

Having changed, the medium started darting about once again. He ran, tumbled, struck the air, seemingly in battle against a mighty opponent. As he fought the unseen force, an assistant placed a heavy bottle and lid on the ritual table. The medium grabbed the bottle in one hand and the lid in the other; he flailed around, his arms moving in great circles over his head and to his sides. Suddenly, he thrust the bottle forward and crashed the lid over its opening. The bottle seemed to take on a life of its own, pulling the medium to the left and then abruptly to the right. Sweat ran down his assistants' faces and chests as they held onto him, keeping him from getting hurt by all the trashing about.

Then, as quickly as the violent movement started, it stopped, as did the music. Mei-hua and the crowd watched, mesmerized, waiting for whatever would happen next.

As if carrying a heavy load, the medium placed the bottle on the table and fell backwards into the arms of his assistants. The battle was over. The medium's spirit won. It captured the water spirit, who was now locked away in the bottle. Exhausted from the strenuous battle, the medium's breath came in gulps. His assistants remained at his side in case they were needed.

After a few moments, the medium moved to the table and took up the brush. He dabbed it into the ink already prepared for him. With rapid, confident, strokes, he wrote out a talisman on a strip of paper. It would protect Ping-an from future threats by any water spirit. Like the characters on the procession's flags, the talisman was written in a unique spirit language which could not be deciphered or understood by humans.

Another assistant handed the medium a cluster of incense sticks, which he took and placed in the bowl along with the first three. Praying, he held his hands together in front of his chest and bowed several times. Mei-hua struggled to see how many sticks were in the bowl. She counted twelve. They represented the months of the year which would all be filled with peace and harmony. It was a blessing for Ping-an, the family, and the household.

Finally, the medium, still possessed, took up the bottle once more. He turned, and as he did the gongs and stringed instruments started up again. Mei-hua put a hand over her right ear to protect it against the music which reverberated off the courtyard's walls. The men regrouped into a line with a flag in the front and at the rear; the medium stood in the center holding the bottle out in front of him. With great fan-fare and a lot of noise they marched out of the courtyard and the Hsu compound. They were taking the trapped water spirit away and would bury it in a field out in the countryside, where it couldn't hurt anyone again.

CHAPTER 16

THE NEXT DAY, Orchid reported to Madam Wu that Ping-an had become noticeably better after the spirit ceremony. Her color was better, with more pink in her cheeks. She showed more willingness to eat something and was able to sit up against pillows.

Mei-hua had mixed feelings. She hadn't observed any remarkable change in Ping-an, although there had been steady improvement even before the spirit medium came and performed his rites. Her young mistress was eating more, but that was not saying much. A mouse would eat more. Still, she was glad Ping-an's mother no longer held her responsible.

One day Ping-an, still fragile and listless, pushed herself up into a sitting position, pulled her silk jacket more closely around her thin frame, and called Mei-hua to her bedside.

"Mama says you saved my life by reading the note I left and running to get my brother to help. Thank you."

Mei-hua bowed deeply to show her respect for the young mistress.

"Come and sit here, next to my bed," Ping-an said, pointing to a small stool near her. "You know, I wish I could read and write better. I'm afraid that I'm such a failure that my parents will have a hard time finding a husband from a good family for me."

Mei-hua vigorously shook her head. She'd been thinking of Ping-an's inability to write even the simplest characters well, and she'd reached a conclusion: she could help her little mistress learn to write better. Since Ping-an had brought the subject up herself, this was the best time to introduce the idea.

Mei-hua rose from the stool and walked over to a small writing table pushed up against the wall. She took an inkstick and started rubbing it over Ping-an's inkstone while mixing in a bit of water. She made a nice, dark, rich liquid. Intrigued, Ping-an stretched forward to see what her maid was doing.

Mei-hua put the ink on a bed tray next to a brush and blank sheet of rice paper and brought everything over to her mistress. As she placed the tray on Ping-an's lap, she mimed taking up the brush and writing.

"Oh, no! I can't write!" Ping-an squealed in a high-pitched voice. "You saw my note. My characters are pathetic. No, I don't want to do this." She shook her head and raised her shoulders to turn away.

Mei-hua was not easily dissuaded. She picked up the brush and put it into her mistress's hand.

Ping-an sighed. "What can I say? You saved my life; I can write something for you." Without another word, she took the brush and dipped it into the ink. "What would you like?"

Immediately, Mei-hua understood Ping-an's critical

error, which destroyed her penmanship. She held the brush at an angle, causing her to lose control of the movement of the soft bristles. Instead of clean, strong lines, she produced uneven smudges.

With a firm yet gentle hand, Mei-hua changed her brush position until the brush handle pointed straight up.

"You mean to hold it like this? But I've always done it the other way," Ping-an said.

Mei-hua ignored her. By pretending to write herself, she encouraged Ping-an to begin writing. As soon as she began, her brush slipped back into a slanted position. Mei-hua again smoothly corrected the slant, then lightly held her hand over Ping-an's as she helped her trace out *ping*, "peace."

Ping-an laughed out loud when they finished the character. "Orchid! Come over here and look at what I've written!"

Orchid and the two young maids hurried over to the bed. Each of the three exclaimed over how well she wrote the word.

Mei-hua smiled. She was glad Ping-an felt successful at writing even one character, because now she no longer felt so hopeless and would be more willing to practice and study,.

"Let's do another one, Mei-hua," Ping-an said with a giggle.

Grinning, Mei-hua guided her young mistress's hand in writing *an*, "quiet."

"My name! Look how well I wrote my name." Ping-an turned to Mei-hua with a sparkle in her eyes. "This is the best I've ever done."

Mei-hua again made a writing motion, encouraging Ping-an to continue.

"What shall I write now?"

The bondmaid passed her hand back and forth over the two characters written out on the paper.

"Do these again? Okay. By myself? All right, I'll try, but don't expect too much."

Tentatively, Ping-an held the brush over the beautiful white rice paper. Mei-hua held her own hand out as if she had a brush standing straight up and down in her hand. Ping-an studied her hand, corrected her own, then checked for Mei-hua's approval. The maid nodded encouragement and the young mistress slowly started forming the character *ping*.

After this lesson, the two young women worked together every day writing characters. Each day Mei-hua taught her something new in forming a line or properly making the ink. Writing became an art, not a chore, for Ping-an. Mei-hua delighted in her progress. From the beginning Mei-hua believed her mistress had the ability to write well, because her hand work, such as her finely detailed embroidery and her paintings, were graceful and creative. Ping-an's hidden talent began to blossom. While Mei-hua liked Teacher Song, she realized his harsh treatment of his student incapacitated her and made her stumble even more. Hating school, Ping-an acted out her dislike by being inattentive and careless.

On one especially long rainy afternoon, Ping-an asked Mei-hua if she had learned to play chess. Ping-an usually played with Orchid, but today Madam Wu ordered the older maid to come to her rooms and help serve several guests she had invited to play board games.

Mei-hua nodded her head "yes" and smiled brightly. Ping-an had never asked her before, so she never played. As it happened, chess was her favorite game.

She and her father used to play quite often. Neither Orchid nor Ping-an were very good players, but she didn't care. Now she could join in the fun.

"Get the board and set it up at the table near the window. I want to get out of bed for a while today," Ping-an said.

Mei-hua paused. She gave her young mistress a questioning glance.

"It's no problem. I can get up for a bit. Besides, the table is only a few feet from my bed," she said smiling.

They had just begun when Ping-an realized her bondservant had more than a passing knowledge of the game.

"Why didn't you tell me you were an expert at this, too?" she teased. Then, realizing what she had said, she glanced up at Mei-hua and both girls began laughing.

The friendship between them grew each day as they studied together, amused themselves with board games, and even played charades with the other maids in the room. Because of her lively portrayal and playfulness, Mei-hua was a favorite for acting out phrases or names.

Ping-an insisted Mei-hua sleep in her rooms rather than return to the maid's quarters. As a result, Guei-lung could now visit her and ply her with his well-intentioned but prying questions. Although Mei-hua trusted Guei-lung, she was afraid he would eventually manage to learn all of her secrets. She had to protect herself, and to do so she needed to avoid Guei-lung and his inquisitiveness completely. Fortunately, the doctor insisted Ping-an have few visitors in order to keep her quiet, which also restricted her brother's visits. On the few occasions he did come to the room, Mei-hua disappeared into the maids' quarters, where men were not allowed.

In spite of this relative period of comfort and peace, the constant drum beat of uncertainly undermined it all. Mei-hua never forgot that Master Hsu might begin questioning her again at any time. So far, though, his work demanded his full attention. As a result, he came into his private chambers late and left early every morning. He rarely had a moment to stop in Ping-an's room and, when he did, his visits were quite short. He never paid any particular attention to the bondservant or any of the other maids. Mei-hua, on the other hand, did learn more about him and his work. As she had suspected, he held the position of magistrate for the Court. The same as her father. The servants gossiped about how he had an important, though mysterious, case which they claimed could make his career.

Even though Mei-hua began to think of Ping-an more as a student and friend, she was also keenly aware of the temporary nature of the happy security of these rooms.

CHAPTER 17

PING-AN SAT sharing breakfast with her mother. This morning she radiated health, with her ebony hair swept into a large, loose bun on top of her head. The peach and green flowered silk skirt and matching jacket she wore further highlighted her cheeks' delicate, glowing color. Mei-hua and the other maids moved quietly in and out of the room carrying tea and small dishes of food. Another couple of maids stood near the side wall waiting for orders. Madam Wu held up an envelope and flicked it in the air.

"My dear, I just received word from your Aunt Xi. She is holding a special celebration for the Shàngsì festival this year."

"Oh, good!" Ping-an clapped her hands in delight. "When is it? When will we go and how long will we stay?" She loved parties. They always meant a change of pace and a chance to visit, gossip, and play games.

Her mother smiled at her. "With your illness,"—Madam Wu never referred to her daughter's suicide attempt directly—"you've lost track of so many things. Tomorrow is the first day of the third month. The Shàngsì festival is only three days away! We'll have to leave as soon as everything's packed. Aunt Xi especially wants us to attend the celebration's beginnings which will start early on the first day, and we'll stay with her for two nights before returning home."

Ping-an beamed. "This'll be so much fun. I can't wait to see my cousins. And Aunt Xi and Gran'ma Fei, too, of course!" A frown crossed her face. "But why are they celebrating Shàngsì this year?" Ping-an sat across from her Mother on the kang. She took up a plum from a shallow translucent porcelain bowl and nibbled thoughtfully. "I don't remember her having a party last year."

Madam Wu sadly nodded her head. "Gran'ma Fei has not been well these past two months. Your Aunt Xi is a devout Daoist and believes the Shàngsì festival is an important time to get rid of the five evils and of restoring health and well-being."

Ping-an squinted trying to recall what she'd heard about the festival. "The five evils. I can't remember what they all are," she said.

"How can you be so forgetful? Sometimes I worry about you."

Ping-an silently looked down at her hands.

Mei-hua nervously watched, waiting for what Madam Wu would say next. Although Ping-an was much improved, her friend feared she would try suicide again if she became too upset.

Madam Wu quickly shook her head. "It's that

medicine you're still on. I think it's time you stopped taking it." Then, returning to their original conversation, she said, "The five evils are the snake, scorpion, centipede, spider, and toad."

"I thought Double Five, the fifth day of the fifth month, marked the time of the five evils," Ping-an said.

Her mother smiled. "You're right. Double Five is an important date, but Shàngsì is as well, especially here in the south. And, most importantly, Aunt Xi wants to celebrate it, so we will, too."

Mei-hua listened with interest. She was quite familiar with the Shàngsì festival because it was celebrated widely in Changsha, where she lived with her father. There, people used many amulets and hung pictures of the ghost chaser, Zhong-kui, to ward off the evil spirits and to protect their families. Sometimes she wished she had an image of Zhong-kui to put up in her mistress's room.

Madam Wu went on. "Aunt Xi wants to do all she can to help Gran'ma Fei recover, so she is having a Daoist priest and his helpers come to chase away any evil influences in the house. They've told her the Shàngsì festival is an important time for the family to get together and show strength in turning away those bad spirits and supporting the good and positive. After the rituals, we'll all celebrate by eating and being together."

Although Mei-hua's father never indulged in such Daoist rituals, she understood why they were important to both Ping-an's aunt and mother. Gran'ma Fei's health was at stake and one didn't take chances at such a time. Every possibility for restoring and maintaining her health had to be taken seriously.

Mei-hua wondered what they did during the ritual

and festival. With the establishment of the new Ming Dynasty, not many Han people celebrated Shàngsì anymore. Many considered it to be an ethnic minority festival. While the government didn't actually discourage people from celebrating it, they clearly discounted it as unimportant to the Nation.

"Well, this celebration will be good for Gran'ma Fei and we'll all have a lot of fun!" Ping-an said with a toss of her head. "I'll wear my new jacket and my new hair pin."

Madam Wu laughed, happy to see her daughter behaving like her old self.

"Oh, one slight change," her mother said. "This year your brother won't be with us." Madam Wu smoothed out her skirt. Before Ping-an could argue, she waved her objection aside and said, "He's too old to be with the women. He'll stay with Uncle Fei's boys and the other men."

At Ping-an's downcast face, she added, "We'll be together for the party; but he won't sleep in the same courtyard with us."

Ping-an brightened. "Do you remember the Mid-Autumn Festival celebration they had three years ago? Remember?"

Her mother smiled. "Yes, you and all your cousins each had a lantern to hold up over the pond. You all looked so lovely."

Ping-an laughed, "Until Guei-lung fell in trying to catch a frog!" And with that, she reminisced about the past and the prospects for this year's parties.

"Since Gran'ma Fei's still recovering, I suspect this celebration will be more subdued and less elaborate than her past parties. But never mind. Once the Shàngsì rituals and celebration are complete and her health is better, things will return to normal," her mother said. "In the meantime, because of her delicate condition, I've decided we shouldn't bring along too many extra servants. You may take two of your maids. Perhaps Orchid and Mei-hua."

Ping-an shot Mei-hua a grin. Her mother had noticed how her daughter had improved in health and in attitude. Even she realized at least some of this change was due to her new maid. This had to be why she took the unusual step of allowing Mei-hua to accompany her daughter on the visit rather than one of the more senior maids.

Mei-hua smiled back, although she felt ambivalent about going. She had grown to truly like Ping-an, and she knew they would enjoy the Shàngsì Festival celebrations. Still, if she remained here, the virtually empty house would provide her with her best opportunity for escape. No matter how much she cared for Ping-an and her family, Mei-hua never lost sight of her need to flee before Master Hsu discovered her identity.

The next couple of days passed quickly in preparation for the trip. Madam Wu even ordered a new outfit for Mei-hua. Although Ping-an always wore pastel colors, she picked out a shimmering jewel-toned blue-green silk for Mei-hua with a matching purple scarf. The colors brought out her large, dark eyes. Delighted, Mei-hua looked forward to wearing the beautiful clothes.

When the day came to leave for Aunt Xi's house, the servants loaded several trunks of clothing and gifts onto a cart. A line of brightly polished palanquins stood ready: one for Madam Wu, another for Ping-an and Mei-hua, and three more for Orchid and the other maids Madam Wu decided she needed on this three day visit.

The men would come later. Master Hsu's duties did not allow him to leave with his wife and daughter. Guei-lung would wait with his father.

Riding the short distance to Aunt Xi's, the curtains to the palanquins were closed tightly against the street scene, as they should be for decorous women of official or wealthy households. Nonetheless, Mei-hua and Ping-an managed to each create a little peephole between the curtain and the side of the chair. Ping-an whispered excitedly about the people and shops they passed as they were carried through the crowded street. Mei-hua giggled her silent giggle. She was truly enjoying the trip.

Except for these infrequent visits to relative's houses, Ping-an never left the Hsu compound. Before Mei-hua's own disastrous trip with her faithful servants, she had never been allowed to wander outside of her father's house either. Girls were guarded, protected at all times, and the easiest way to do this was to keep them home.

In no time at all, the servants carried the palanquin parade through a pair of massive double wooden doors set inside substantial, protective walls enclosing the Fei home and park-like gardens. Once inside, they continued across the sprawling outer courtyard. Large pots set in rows were filled with small trees that were just beginning to bud. Even before entering the women's quarters, Mei-hua could hear feminine voices and excited, animated chatter. Four ladies with a group of maids came toward the palanquins as Madam Wu and her party dismounted into a lush spring garden. Along with the beaming women, the fragrance of freshly turned earth greeted them. Examining their hostesses' faces, Mei-hua had no doubt that they were Ping-an's relatives as they called out to her and her mother. Within moments Aunt Xi and her three daughters surrounded them with a glowing cheerful welcome, taking their arms and leading them onto the surrounding veranda.

They shared tea with their aunt and cousins in a large, overcrowded room. Scenic scrolls hung on the walls; glazed pots with colorful flowers and miniature trees sat in clusters on elaborately carved wood tables of various sizes and heights. Mei-hua stood along the wall with the other maids, in attendance but unobtrusive. She carefully observed the aunt and her daughters as they interacted with Madam Wu and Ping-an. At the same time, the question of whether this new family would be helpful or detrimental in her learning the whereabouts of her father's friend and the family she was to stay with played through her thoughts as she observed and analyzed.

After a while, Madam Wu, her daughter, and their attendants were shown to the guest quarters. Madam Wu and Ping-an each had their own rooms while the maids slept together in the back of the compound. At Ping-an's request, a small cot was brought into her room for Mei-hua.

Once the servants finished unpacking the trunks and putting away the clothing, shoes, and other accessories, Madam Wu ordered everyone to rest until dinner. Ping-an, who was always rather weak and tired easily, fell silent almost as soon as she laid her head down.

Mei-hua lay wide awake. The soft sound of steady breathing told her Ping-an had fallen asleep. No longer hearing voices coming from the other guest rooms, Mei-hua rose and stepped noiselessly to the door. Peering out onto the courtyard's garden, she was again aware of the wealth of this large, extended family she'd become a part of. Imposing pale green pots with rare specimens of diminutive trees and spring plants stood like soldiers on either side of a narrow, carefully designed path of flat stepping stones. The walkway artfully meandered through the garden courtyard leading visitors past a series of twisting, towering rocks that seemed to spring out of the ground like geysers of stone. Their convoluted shapes punctuated with holes held places of honor along the path. Mei-hua recognized these rocks as coming from Tai Shan, the most important mountain in China. Like the mountain, these stones were also considered to be sacred and were, therefore, highly sought after.

Further into the garden, a half-moon bridge arched over a tiny stream linking two shallow pools of water. Mei-hua could make out the flashing gold of carp swimming just beneath the water's surface. Simple wooden benches with marble seats were placed around the garden, offering visitors a chance to sit and rest. Everything appeared to be perfect. Clearly, Mei-hua thought, this family is blessed. But then, she used to think she was fortunate, too. She and her father. Now everything was dust. Worse. She stopped, caught up in her own thoughts, her own worries. *How was she to get out? Could she protect her father and their extended family?* She moaned softly. What could she do?

As she stood thinking and gazing out at the beautiful garden, a slight motion behind a large willow tree on the far side of the courtyard caught her eye. Could someone else be wandering through the garden? But when she looked again, straining to see into the depths, there was no one.

Curious, she cautiously strolled around the path, as if leisurely enjoying the garden. Admiring this plant or that rock, she made her way toward the willow tree. When she reached it and passed under it, she felt the tug of low hanging braches as they gripped the shoulder and side of her long silk jacket. She stopped and carefully disengaged the brushwood. Madam Wu would not be amused if she came back with holes in the silk. It took several minutes to remove the offending twigs without leaving tears in the material.

Once free, she gazed around the tree but saw no one. She was alone.

She remained hidden behind the willow's sweeping branches while she continued to examine the area. Soon she spied a plain wooden storage shed. Next to it sat a strong but roughly made wooden door in the compound's impressive stone wall. After a quick glance around, she rapidly moved toward the small gate while keeping an eye out for anyone who might see her.

She carefully pulled on the door to see if it was locked. The craggy, pine slab easily gave way. She held it slightly ajar and squinted through the opening. To her surprise, it led directly onto a public street. An old man sleeping peacefully against the wall was the sole guard. In her own home and at Ping-an's, every outside entrance had at least two watchmen. She'd never heard of an outside door leading directly into the living quarters. A chill spread through her as she realized how vulnerable such an arrangement made Ping-an and her mother, even as they rested peacefully in rooms off this courtyard.

She put her hand on her jade amulet as it lay against her skin. No heat, no danger—at least not to her. In the past, the amulet had warned her of trouble. Now, she wished it could just give her advice.

She remained in place, still seeking guidance from her jade. Then the reassuring voice spoke to her: "The wise person must consider both advantages and disadvantages equally. Through recognizing potential gain in a bad situation, problems can be solved."

She looked around, relieved that the jade was advising her again. *Right, but why? What was going to happen?* The jade remained cool. If the situation was not harmful to her, perhaps her mistress was in danger? Why? This door had been here, just as it is—leading right onto the public street and with an unreliable guard—probably since the house was built years ago. What was different now?

Shutting the door firmly, Mei-hua latched its one small hook. *A flimsy lock for such a prominent household*, she thought. Then she went over to the shed and peeked in. It revealed little. A few pieces of well-used work clothes hung from wall pegs. She surmised the clothes belonged to the household's errand boy when he went outside the house to take messages or make purchases for the family. Garden tools lined the walls as well. At least this seemed normal enough.

Realizing she'd been roaming for some time without figuring out what her jade was telling her, Mei-hua stealthily returned to Ping-an's room and lay down. If Madam Wu caught a glimpse of her wandering through the compound during rest period, she would wonder why.

Later, when dressing for the evening celebrations, Ping-an insisted Mei-hua wear her new clothing, even though the Shàngsì festival's celebration started that evening after the daylong rituals were complete. The young mistress also gave her a long purple silk sash to wear around her waist and an inexpensive but intricately carved iridescent shell comb for her hair.

"Well, we have you looking lovely," Ping-an said. "Although there's not much we can do about your shoes."

Mei-hua frowned.

"I'm not criticizing," her mistress quickly asserted. "It's just that we don't have any other shoes to replace those blue felt ones you normally wear." Ping-an shook her head.

In fact, with a brief peek at Ping-an's artfully embroidered tiny shoes, even Mei-hua had to admit her own shoes seemed rather ugly. It's not important, she told herself. I have my mother's feet: unbound and strong.

As Mei-hua waited on Ping-an during the noon meal and at the card party later, she was keenly aware of Guei-lung's mischievous eyes following her. At one point, he stopped her immediately outside the door as she left the room to get more refreshments for the guests.

"You're stunning, Mei-hua, really beautiful," he whispered close to her ear.

She bowed to him, as if he were just a master complimenting her as a servant. Still, in spite of herself, she realized she was blushing. She was also conscious of how handsome and mature he appeared in his gray silk tunic. Once again her muteness saved her from having to say anything. *Being unable to speak has its advantages*, she thought with relief.

"You don't have to bow to me." He teased. "We're friends, remember. We saved Ping-an together. That means we share a special tie; we're bonded to each other," he said grinning.

She grinned back. He was so disarming when he smiled.

He reached out to touch her hand, but she stepped away. At the same time, Precious Virtue, Madam Wu's senior maid, came dashing through the door.

"Mei-hua, what are you doing? Get going! They're waiting for their tea!" Almost within the same instant, she noticed Guei-lung. "So, you're causing her to delay. Leave her alone, she has work to do. You'll get her into trouble with your Mama."

Mei-hua didn't hear the rest of her comments because she'd already fled to the kitchen to retrieve more hot water for tea.

The card party broke up in time for everyone to enjoy a heavy evening meal. With so much activity and food, adults and children alike retired late, exhausted and ready for a deep sleep.

Everyone except Mei-hua. She could not help but think of the door opening onto the public street. Was the old man still on guard? Was he awake?

She lay on her cot. The cotton of her dark tunic pulled tightly against her as she turned over. She grabbed it and tugged, forcing it to release its grip. Once free of the entangling tunic, she lay on her back, rigid from worry and staring into the darkness. After some time, as she finally started to relax, she heard the soft sound of felt shoes moving over the veranda's wooden plank floor. She listened more intently. Were those voices? She waited.

"Here. In here."

"Wait, you fool! There are two of them in the room.

Mei-hua froze. Her mouth felt dry; she couldn't swallow. There were strangers outside their door!

"One's the bondmaid," the gruff voice continued. "She can't talk, so don't worry about her. Just tie her up. Get the magistrate's daughter as fast as you can. Cover her mouth, wrap her in this, and throw her over your shoulder until we get outside the gate. The cart will be waiting; no one will notice a thing. Got it? Okay, let's go."

Mei-hua turned over and lay facing the door so she could see them as they came into the room. Three men entered. One pointed to Ping-an and directed a broad shouldered man to go over to her. Tapping a second, thinner, man on the shoulder, he pointed to Mei-hua. Crouching to keep a low profile, he started for her.

Before he got to her, however, Mei-hua sprang from the cot and grabbed a vase sitting on a nearby table. Screaming at the top of her lungs, she brought the vase down on the man's head. As he fell to the floor, Mei-hua called out, "Ping-an!"

Startled by the unexpected commotion, the other two men momentarily paused, confused.

"Kidnapers! Ping-an's in danger! Kidnappers!" Mei-hua screamed as she threw another vase, this time at the man approaching Magistrate Hsu's daughter.

Ping-an started up, saw the men, and screamed with such vehemence Mei-hua was sure she could be heard in Beiping, hundreds of miles away.

Mei-hua leapt toward the leader and delivered a side kick to his chest. Slamming hard against the wall, the stunned thug called to his men.

"Forget them. Let's get out of here," he yelled, scrambling for the door.

As suddenly as it all began, the struggle ended. The men fled through the garden, running straight toward the door behind the willow tree. Mei-hua stood panting and watched several men from the household run through the door, chasing after the would-be kidnapers. Madam Wu, Madam Fei, Orchid, Precious Virtue, and several other women rushed to calm Ping-an.

For a brief moment Mei-hua was forgotten, but she was painfully aware that her cover was gone. They knew she was able to speak, and would soon realize she had martial arts training. Questions were sure to follow. Madam Wu was suspicious before, but now she would be unrelenting. As would her husband.

The words, *Discover the advantage in a bad situation*, reverberated in her head.

Looking around, she realized the garden was empty: the men had run after the intruders and the women were tending to Ping-an.

She moved swiftly, running to the willow tree. She glanced behind her and towards the guest windows. No one. Slipping into the shed, she stuffed her fine cotton clothing into a large pottery jar and put on the errand boy's rough pants and jacket. She stuffed her hair into his cap, ignoring its grimy appearance. Her hands shook. The amulet's warmth against her skin alerted her to be cautious.

She paused to gather her resolve, then took a deep breath and straightened up. Remembering Guei-lung's earlier comments about her walk, she forced herself to carefully mimic a worker's gait, and sauntered out of the shed, through the door, and into the crowded street. At last, she was free

She stopped outside the gate to study the night street and the few people who were gathering around, drawn by the commotion. By now her amulet felt hot, but as she examined the street, everyone seemed to be minding their own business. No one paid any attention to just another street urchin. *My amulet probably feels hot because I'm stressed*, she thought. *But now I'm free. Free.* She couldn't stop thinking of the word and how beautifully it rolled around on her tongue. It was all she could do to keep from laughing out loud. Before she celebrated though, she had to put some distance between herself and this house.

She turned to mingle with the crowd when she felt a strong hand seize her shoulder in a vise-like grip.

"Just where do you think you're going, you little thief," a deep, stern voice demanded.

Oh, no. Not again. Looking up, her heart sank. She was in the hands of a police officer!

CHAPTER 18

THE MUSCULAR OFFICER lifted her so high her flailing feet couldn't touch the ground. She began to panic. Within seconds, however, the powerful smell of his garlic breath brought her crashing back to earth.

"The magistrate will be happy with what I've caught here!" he sputtered into her face. His vise-like grip tightened even more as he dropped her onto the road.

"Stop wriggling," he said, giving her a firm shake before dragging her toward the mansion's garden gate.

"We've got one! We've got one!" an excited voice called out down the street. Quicker than a swarm of locusts devouring a field, a crowd of people appeared from out of doorways and alleyways, all rushing toward the voice. As if by magic, everyone knew what had happened within the courtyard and they were all determined to get a view of the culprit. This was the best free show they had had in weeks. No one was to be denied their share of the excitement.

During the ensuing crush and noise of people pushing forward to catch a glimpse of the captured criminal, a man stumbled into the officer holding Mei-hua, causing him to also lose his balance. He lurched sideways and, as he struggled to keep from falling, momentarily relaxed his grip on Mei-hua. Without thought, she violently twisted her body, freeing herself.

"What the...?" the officer yelled, his hand shooting out to grab her.

His fingers closed on dusty night air. Cursing, he started to run after Mei-hua's slight form disappearing into the crowd. He shoved and pushed against the mass of people, yelling at them to get out of the way for an officer of the law, but their sheer numbers packed into the narrow street slowed him down. It seemed he had lost her.

Mei-hua moved forward, dodging and ducking in and around the surging throng. Her small size made it easier for her to pass through, but it didn't take her long to realize that actually getting out of this crowd would take some time, and by then the police officer might find her again.

She glanced at the multiple doorways lining the alley. One door stood open leading to a darkened space. A place to hide. Breathless, she darted inside. At first, she saw nothing in the lightless room, although a heady fragrance of camphor and sandalwood filled the air. She must be in a carpenter's shop, or perhaps a furniture store.

Straining to penetrate the inky interior, her eyes slowly adjusted and the vague shapes around her began to make sense. Piles of wood several feet high filled one side of the room; large work tables and small wooden stools clustered together on the other. A carpenter's shop. A perfect place to disappear for a while.

She smiled. She could not have chosen a better hiding place if she had planned it. For a brief moment, the camphor fragrance reminded her of home. Nanny kept the family clothes safe from one season to the next in camphor wood trunks. Her smile died on her lips. Would she ever return to her own home and the simple patterns of daily life again?

Just then, a rasping voice boomed outside the door. "Have you seen a young ruffian about so tall running through here?"

The police officer!

Quickly, soundlessly, Mei-hua inserted herself into a pile of camphor boards, lowering her body down into a squatting position. She hoped her dark trousers and shirt merged with the darkness, camouflaging her as they blended into the deep shadows cast by the substantial wood piles.

She tugged at a short piece of board to cover her face. Shifting her weight onto her right leg, she tried to adjust her left foot; another board pressed painfully into her left ankle. If she could just slide her foot a little more to the front...

Suddenly, a blaze of light tunneled into the room from outside the doorway. The tall, broad-shouldered police officer entered, holding a torch and banishing the room's cover of darkness. He strode from pile to pile, from table to cupboard, pausing now and then to check more thoroughly behind a hill of cut wood, under a work bench, or into a newly made trunk.

As he passed Mei-hua's camphor boards, he paused and swung his torch around to peer into the wood's crevices. Mei-hua stopped breathing. She didn't dare move despite her awkward position. She bit her cheek to distract herself from the throbbing pain in her ankle.

The officer paused in front of her hiding place. A noise outside in the alley had caught his attention; he stood listening. Her right leg was getting numb from holding all of her weight in this crumpled position. Would he notice if she shifted her weight just a little, only an inch? Yes, of course he would, she chastised herself. *You're almost free*, she told herself. *He's almost past your hiding place. Don't give up now.*

The sound grew louder; rhythmic bongs from a gong reverberated through the air, signaling a criminal was being taken to court. With a final glance around the room, the officer marched to the door and was gone.

Mei-hua waited. She put her hand over her chest and the amulet hidden under her jacket. It radiated a slight warmth. She had to be careful. He might come back. After a short pause, she slowly and painfully moved her left foot away from the aggravating board and shifted her weight so that it rested more evenly on her two sore limbs. A cramp started in her right leg in response to the stress of holding her weight for so long, but there was nothing she could do about it. She remained quiet and alert.

From the sounds outside, she guessed the crowd was breaking up. With relief, she started to straighten up when she heard a shirrr-shirrr-shirrr from across the room. A small lamp's dancing quiet light lit the room. Mei-hua peered through a crevice in the wood pile; a huge shadow moved over the wall.

She froze, fearing the police officer had returned. Motionless, she stopped breathing. But she couldn't quiet her heart. She was sure its traitorous drum beat would reveal her hiding place. He must be able to hear its deafening racket! She listened again for his footsteps.

Silence. Nothing.

Willing her body to disappear, to merge with the camphor wood, she covered her heart with her hand to control its beating.

Shirrr-shirrr-shirrr. The soft sound of felt shoes over wood became louder with each breath.

Silence.

"You can come out now," a voice intoned.

Mei-hua dared to look up. A small but strongly built elderly man stood glaring at her in the wood pile. There was no mistake, she thought; no guessing; no hoping he just thought he saw someone hiding. Someone who might turn out to be no more than a shadow or a ghost. *He knows I am here.* A weight pressed against her chest. *I'm lost. It's over.*

She gradually stood up, disengaging herself from the pile and its excruciating wooden barbs.

"Had a run-in with the police, eh? Come on out. You're okay; he's gone." The man paused, squinting slightly as he looked her over. "I saw you sneak out of the house. Steal anything?"

"No sir, there was trouble in the house and seeing as how I was the newest one there I thought they'd blame me." Mei-hua mimicked the voice, rhythm, and grammar of a young boy she had seen working around the Hsu compound. Wearing the clothing of a laborer, she hoped he'd believe she was a young boy. Through subterfuge she'd control the damage caused by being found. At least this man wouldn't know her real identity, and that might give her some time to figure out what to do next.

"Did you?"

"No, sir! I'd never!" Mei-hua exclaimed, giving her head a vigorous shake.

"Wife! Wife! Come here!"

"What is it, husband?"

"I found this kid running from the police. The officer thinks he's one of the criminals they were looking for tonight. The boy says he's innocent. What do you think?"

A small, thin woman came out of an adjacent room. The scent of onion, garlic, and soy sauce followed her and competed with the camphor fragrance. With a canny eye, she scrutinized the young figure standing near her husband. Her eyes were sharp and her examination thorough, though not unkind.

"What's your name child?"

"Little Big Feet," Mei-hua answered promptly, knowing the local people often used nicknames instead of the names their parents gave them.

The wife laughed. "Okay, 'Little Big Feet', how did you come to be in Magistrate Hsu's household? Are you their bondservant?"

"No, 'mam. Master Peng, the carpenter who works in the big house, found me one day when I was on the street and let me work for him. No money, but I got rice every day." Mei-hua kept her eyes glued to her feet, in an unassertive stance appropriate for a young boy. "But, now I'm afraid they'll blame me for things, because I'm new."

"Master Peng, the carpenter, eh?" the wife repeated. Then glancing at the older man, she continued, "Well, Husband, why not keep him here? You told me this morning you needed an extra set of hands. He can work for you, until you find out more from Master Peng.

"If he's beholden to Master Peng, send him back.

Master Peng would be happy to reward you for finding his apprentice. If he's not beholden to Master Peng, you will have an extra helper. He's no place to go anyhow."

She took Mei-hua's chin in her hand and turned her head back and forth. "He's a bit delicate, but his eyes are clear and he's healthy.

After examining Mei-hua's face, she advised her, "Don't try to run away. The city can be dangerous for the friendless and homeless." Mei-hua nodded; she already knew this to be true.

Finished, the wife turned away and returned to the adjacent room. Mei-hua thought the area had to be their private space with the kitchen. She breathed a sigh of relief. They believed her! They really thought she was a boy, a carpenter's apprentice.

"She likes you. You can stay with us," the carpenter said. "We won't turn you in, but we do need to find out what your situation is."

He waved his hand toward the door his wife had disappeared through, indicating Mei-hua should follow.

After spending the night sleeping on the floor in the carpenter's storage room, Mei-hua rose early and ate a bowl of rice. She spent the day sweeping sawdust and doing other small jobs. Two other men worked for the carpenter: one an older, respected laborer and the second a young fellow who had recently become an apprentice. Based on the employees' comments and her own experience, Mei-hua decided the couple was demanding but kind.

The days passed quickly and Mei-hua lost her fear of living and working within the magistrate's shadow. At the same time, the carpenter trusted her more and more. He no longer watched her every move to make sure she did not run away.

Mei-hua found she actually liked working as a carpenter's helper. She was able to use her voice again— something she rejoiced in daily. She hadn't realized how much she had missed being able to say even the simplest things. And, after a lifetime of living behind high, protective walls, she enjoyed being close to the street and the people who bustled through it. Every activity outside the shop door fascinated her. The traveling troupe of actors performing at the temple across the street was particularly captivating. She was mesmerized by their bright, colorful clothing; high-pitched singing; and clamoring cymbals, gongs, and stringed instruments.

A religious festival, honoring the local temple god, always involved lots of people, noise, and music. A stage had been built outside against the temple wall. Every day the actors put on a play, beginning in the afternoon and going until late at night. Although Mei-hua never left the shop, she ate her evening rice standing in the doorway so she wouldn't miss the excitement. Besides the actors and the music, there were peddlers hawking their wares and noisy banter and laughter from the crowds. Watching the street activity pulled her away from her new duties as often as she dared let it.

Now, however, as she stood eating her evening rice and watching the antics of the jugglers and acrobats performing in the streets, an uneasy feeling came over her. Her amulet started to radiate heat as it lay against her chest. Was someone watching her? Casually, she surveyed the constantly changing crowd moving in and out of the temple's courtyard. Her eyes fell on an enormous, scowling man gazing in her direction. Involuntarily she drew a quick breath as she recognized him: Da Shan! Da Shan, the man her kidnapers had met in Hangzhou just before her attempted escape and recapture by Ben-ji's mother.

The jade still burned her skin causing her to tighten her grip on the rice bowl. A flood of anxiety made it difficult to think clearly.

Trying to regain control, Mei-hua asked herself: *What's he doing here? He's staring at me!* She shook her head to clear her thoughts. *Perhaps he's looking at those jugglers performing on the street in front of the shop. Surely he doesn't recognize me in these boy's clothes...does he?*

CHAPTER 19

CAUSALLY, MEI-HUA STEPPED BACK into the shadow of the doorway. As if attracted by a nearby peddler spewing curses after a boy who had stolen one of his rice balls, she turned away from Da Shan.

After a few moments, she sneaked a fleeting glance in Da Shan's direction. He was gone. He'd left; he'd not realized it was her. Then, with a smug grin, she thought, *Well, how could he recognize me? He saw a boy, not me.*

Relieved, she held her rice bowl close to her lips, scooped up a bit of the delicious glutinous mass with her chop sticks, and absently shoved it in her mouth. Cymbals sounded and Mei-hua stepped forward again as acrobats bounced, tumbled, and jumped through the street for an appreciative audience.

Without warning, an arm encircled her neck clamping her into a tight hold. She tensed as he jerked her backward; her bowl dropped, breaking as it hit the ground and scattering the rice.

"Quite a bag of tricks you have. So, now you are a boy, eh? Well, you can't fool me."

The blood drained from Mei-hua's face and her heart hammered loudly in her chest. He had recognized her.

Through her rising panic, she heard, *Victory can be plucked from defeat when the danger is greatest. Give the appearance of being pulled into the enemy's plans.*

Mei-hua took a deep breath. She had to be bold and lie. Her only chance was to convince him he was wrong.

"I do not know you, sir. Please, let me go. I work here for Master Mu," she said with a heavy country accent.

For a slight second, he paused.

Was he thinking he had made a mistake? She hoped so.

Unfortunately, he quickly recovered. "Ah, you do talk!" He laughed; or rather, a scratchy sound came out of his throat as his lips pulled back showing his yellowed, crooked teeth.

"Don't worry," he continued, "I am not going to sell you the way that idiot Ben-ji and his mother would have. No, instead I will turn you over to the magistrate. There's a reward out for you and I aim to get it."

Self-satisfaction rang in his voice as he was already counting his reward money.

Mei-hua realized there was no turning back. If she didn't act now, all was lost. She remembered Old Lin's martial arts lessons and immediately went into position. In one continuous motion, she relaxed her body, dropped down a bit to regain her balance, covered her right hand with her left for added strength, and slammed her right elbow into Da Shan's rib cage. Caught unaware, Da Shan loosened his hold on her as his body struck the wall behind him.

Mei-hua was as surprised at the force of the blow as he was. Its power came as much from the surge of adrenalin brought on by fear as from Old Lin's training. Nevertheless, as she spun around to flee, Da Shan's hands thrust forward encircling her neck in a tight grip.

Without missing a beat, she went into a squatting pose, reached behind her and grabbed his hands. She whirled around under his arms, breaking his choke hold. Now she had the advantage; his arms were helplessly crossed one over the other. Keeping his hands crossed, she continued to twist them, forcing his elbows to lock together and reducing him to a helpless position.

She completed her defense with a sharp kick to his groin, released his hands, and let him drop to the ground. As he lay crumpled in the dirt, she fled down the street.

She never looked back as she bobbed and dodged through the crowd. At the corner she made a sharp turn and then another at a narrow opening between buildings. Her feet carried her down the alley back to the carpenter's shop. Moving with the caution and agility of a cat on the hunt, she glided inside and, concealed by the shop's shadows, peeked out the front door. Da Shan was gone; she hoped he had followed her false trail down the street. She was confident he didn't see her return to the shop.

"What are you up to, Little Big Feet?"

Startled, Mei-hua jumped and spun around. The carpenter's wife stood near the battered table, hands on hips, scowling.

"Don't bother lying to me. I saw you outside just

now. Who was that bully? What did he want? Are you in trouble? And," the trace of a grin started to soften her stern mouth, "where did you learn to defend yourself like that?"

Mei-hua understood the kindness that lay behind Mrs. Mu Jiang's severe appearance. Suddenly, aware of the jade's coolness as it rested against her, she felt safe and, at the same time, overwhelmed by all that had happened. She needed to trust and confide in someone.

"Mistress, I'll tell you everything. Some of it you may already know."

"Okay. Sit. There's a bit of rice left. You eat while you tell me," she said, taking a ladle and scooping around the bottom of a worn pot sitting on the table. She handed Mei-hua a small, blue and white bowl with a mound of rice piled high in its center.

Mei-hua's eyes smarted as she tried to keep her emotions under control. The simple, straight-forward kindness of this older woman temporarily overcame her. The carpenter's wife witnessed Da Shan's grabbing her and, therefore, she also must have seen one of her precious few rice bowls break on the ground. A small thing, perhaps, but not when the struggling, hard-working couple could count the number of dishes they owned on one hand. Yet, here she was, without casting blame for destroying her property, entrusting Mei-hua with one of the remaining rice bowls. A small thing, yes, but not when you are as poor as this family.

After a few seconds of silence while she ate and got her emotions under control, Mei-hua began. First, she explained why she was impersonating a boy. Mrs. Mu Jiang nodded, without expressing surprise or distress at this dishonesty within the walls of her own home.

With renewed confidence, in the face of Mrs. Mu's

uncritical acceptance of her story, Mei-hua unburdened her heart and told the kindly woman everything. She told of her father sending her to his classmate's home; pretending to be mute; being kidnapped by thieves; working as a servant; and finally, escaping Da Shan's attempt to kidnap her again outside the carpenter shop. At the end, she took the now cool tea colored jade from around her neck as proof of her story. She held it out for Mrs. Mu to see and then slipped it back under her garment. It rested lightly against her skin.

Mrs. Mu listened without comment, nodding her head now and then. When Mei-hua finished her long, involved story the older woman remained silent, as if listening to an inner voice. After a long pause, she said, "I know it is hard to trust government officials or strangers, but I must tell you Hsu Dou-wu has a fair and honest reputation as a magistrate. He searches for the truth, even when it's inconvenient. Wait until Master Mu comes back, then we'll dress you properly and go to court to talk to the magistrate."

Mei-hua's face begin to tingle and her head to throb. One word resounded in her head: *betrayal*. She'd made a mistake in confiding in this person. Clearly, Mrs. Mu Jiang did not understand what Mei-hua just told her. The last thing she expected the carpenter's wife to say was that she should go to the magistrate! Fair or not, he worked for the Emperor. His job was to turn her over to the government and to her father's enemies. He may even use her to capture her father. How could she have been so stupid as to trust this well-intentioned but simple old woman?

CHAPTER 20

BEFORE MEI-HUA HAD TIME to try another escape from the shop, Mrs. Mu had her in the kitchen, heating water for a bath. She chatted as she fed kindling into the fire.

"You must be properly bathed before we present you to the magistrate," she lectured.

Mei-hua grimaced. Even her hair, in spite of the hat she consistently wore, held more sawdust than a full dust bin.

Mrs. Mu went on non-stop, instructing her on washing, cleaning her nails, and fixing her hair. Her assumption that she didn't know the basics of cleanliness irritated Mei-hua and reminded her of her first day in the Hsu household. How could anyone be so ignorant of everyday cleanliness? She allowed Mrs. Mu's stream of admonitions and instructions on each detail of how to bathe to fall harmlessly around her.

Her mind jumped to her impending doom. Through the bathing ordeal, her stomach waged a war with itself, twisting and churning. The meeting with the magistrate loomed over everything. The results were bound to be disastrous.

As they finished the bath, a voice called out from the shop. "Where's my helper? Why isn't he working?" Mr. Mu had returned.

"Finish rinsing your hair," Mrs. Mu instructed as she wiped her hands across her apron. "I'll talk to my husband.

"Don't worry, Little Big Feet, it'll be all right." With that, Mrs. Mu was out the door and Mei-hua stood abandoned in a puddle of grimy water, wet and shivering in spite of the relative warmth of the room.

Although she remained still and listened intently, only an occasional, indistinct murmur came from the shop. Was the quiet discussion a good or bad sign? Did it mean Master Mu accepted the strange story his wife must now be telling him, or was he merely waiting for her to come out of the kitchen to punish her? Punish her for deceiving them, for being a criminal (why else did the police officer chase her?), and for possibly getting them into trouble because she lived in their home. As with the Hsu household, her presence here created a serious legal threat for the carpenter couple; they could lose their shop to the government and go to jail—if they were lucky.

The hushed voices stopped; no sound came from the adjoining room. Mei-hua finished rinsing her hair. She squeezed her silky, ebony strands, letting the water fall back into the deep wooden bucket. After a final rub with a thin, dusky towel, she put on a simple, dark cotton robe Mrs. Mu left for her, and combed the snarls out of her waist-length hair before tying it back. There was no window in the room and only one door, from which came an intermittent, soft murmur set between long periods of silence. She had no choice but to wait and try to calm her churning stomach. If she needed to take action, there would be time later. She hoped.

Dressed, Mei-hua sat and reflected on her situation. She had been in the stifling room for quite a while. Should she try to go out or remain here? She was about to go into the shop when the soft shirrr-shirrr-shirrr of felt soled boots caught her attention. They stopped outside the closed door. Next, a male voice mumbled something but, again, it was too low for her to understand what he said. She waited.

"Little Big-foot, are you dressed?" Mrs. Mu asked through the door.

"Yes, Mistress," Mei-hua said.

"Then, come out here. We've something to show you."

Mei-hua slowly opened the door and stepped out, not knowing what to expect. She was unprepared for what she saw.

Mr. Mu stood in front of his wife. Mei-hua scanned his face. He appeared serious but not angry. At least, that's what Mei-hua wanted to believe.

"Little Big-foot, my wife here told me your curious story," Mr. Mu said. Then, looking more closely at her, he continued, "Your being a girl came as quite a surprise." He inspected her with a careful eye. "Your work here's been very adequate. As good as any boy's," he added as if a compliment.

She started to relax.

Then, with a thin smile he said, "However, as you can guess, the fact that you are the one the magistrate's hunting for is not so good." He shook his head, but then with a twinkle in his eyes, a real smile crossed his lips. "You've provided us with more surprises than we've had in all of our years."

Mei-hua hesitated. Did this mean he wasn't angry with her; wasn't afraid of being entangled in the courts? She shifted uneasily. Even so, what did he intend to do? Send her back to the magistrate, to the court, as his wife wanted?

"We have the appropriate clothing for you to wear before the court. The silk merchant next door happened to have something you could use," he said, moving away from his wife and exposing a stunning outfit hanging from her right arm. She held a silk skirt with a green-on-green geometric design and a pale gold jacket embroidered with blue flowers and emerald green vines trailing over its front panel.

Mei-hua gasped at the dazzling outfit. She guessed it would cost the humble couple more than a year's income. How could this simple carpenter and his wife ever afford to purchase such a wardrobe? Why would they?

"I couldn't possibly...," Mei-hua began.

"Never mind, child," Mr. Mu said. "You must appear before the Judge in your finest, if you're to impress him. He must realize he's not dealing with an insignificant, indentured servant girl. If you wear this dress, he'll see you for who you are—that you come from an important family—and he'll be more lenient with you."

Still, panic gripped Mei-hua and she threw herself onto her knees in front of him. "Please, don't make me go to the magistrate! I'll leave you and the shop without anyone knowing who I am!"

"No, Little Big-foot. That's impossible. You can't

leave and think no one will notice. People already know I've an apprentice; they'll ask questions if you just disappear."

Mei-hua's heart sank.

"Besides, you can't run away forever. From what my wife tells me, you've no family here. You're alone. Without family to protect you, where could you go?" He took her hand and helped her stand.

"I know of your special skills. Mrs. Mu told me of the "unfortunate" bully who tried to take you away," he said, trying to sound amused to ease her fears. "Nevertheless, believe me, this is best. We'll help as much as we can. If you tell your story well, you'll find Magistrate Hsu to be a fair judge.

"Don't be afraid. Fear is unbecoming to one such as you," he said, adding, "And who knows? You may even be reunited with your father once more."

"But the clothing," Mei-hua started, hoping to find a way to delay the inevitable, "it must have cost..."

"Don't worry about these old things," Mrs. Mu said slightly swaying the skirt and jacket in her arms. "We're able to get them from our neighbor, Mr. Tang. He sewed them for a customer who never paid him, so he was stuck with them. What could he do?" she asked. "He had to dump them someplace."

Mrs. Mu's disparaging remarks about the worth of their gift to her didn't fool Mei-hua. Her comments about the clothing being "old" and having to be "dumped" someplace was simply standard, polite modesty. They paid dearly for them, and did so out of the goodness of their hearts. Just so she could present herself in the best possible light before the magistrate. Mei-hua straightened her shoulders. Well, if they were willing to put so much of their own meager funds into her going, she would go proudly and with confidence. Maybe. Right now she did not feel very confident. Nevertheless, she bowed low once again. "I am profoundly thankful for your kindness to this unworthy person." Her "thank you" was standard, even formulaic, but today she truly meant every word.

"The court's adjourned at this time for lunch. You'll use your time wisely if you go inside to dress and prepare your hair." Mr. Mu stopped and looked thoughtfully at her long, loose locks. "Of course, you could always wear it hidden in your hat, as you usually do." His eyes twinkled with mirth.

Mei-hua grinned at the comical image of her dressed in the beautiful silk skirt and jacket and wearing her hair pushed up under a worker's hat.

"Never you mind, husband," Mrs. Mu broke in. "I'll help her to get ready. You just wait and see what'll come out." With that, she herded Mei-hua back into the kitchen.

Mei-hua sat on a low wooden stool as the older woman combed, parted, and formed her hair into two high buns on either side of her head.

"This'll influence his eminence, the magistrate. This is the old Chinese Han style, and is popular amongst the people. You don't want to remind him of the non-Chinese Mongol rule, of the Yuan Dynasty from whose yoke our blessed emperor has freed us. You want to look every bit the daughter of a Chinese scholar. Which, of course, you are."

Mei-hua nodded, impressed at the political sophistication of this common working woman. But then, this was Hangzhou, the old national capital, and people here were much more aware of power, as well as its temporary and fragile nature. How could she have doubted this experienced old woman's wisdom?

Finally, after much preparation and many requests to Mr. Mu to bring this box and that to the door, Mei-hua was properly and exquisitely dressed. Mrs. Mu wrapped a gold sash around the top of the shimmering green skirt as a belt. The two ends bowed in front and hung down past her knees. Another red ribbon with two ornamental knots placed on either side of a piece of circular, lettuce-green jade dangled on the side of her sash. Mrs. Mu wanted her to wear the jade for good luck.

After some time, Mrs. Mu stepped back to admire her handiwork. She examined Mei-hua with great care and a critical eye. With a slight frown, she shook her head.

"My dear, there're two more items you need before you're ready. First, there's the matter of your feet."

Mei-hua blushed. She never regretted having her feet unbound; still, she hated being reminded over and over of how big they appeared to others. Looking over at the straw sandals which she usually wore around the shop, she was aware they were completely wrong and out-of-place with such a fine dress. What alternative was there? They were all she had.

"In the past, I wore simple felt shoes, which I embroidered with flowers and butterflies. Since I doubt this type of shoe can be found here, perhaps just plain shoes would do. If we can find them in a light color," Mei-hua suggested.

Mrs. Mu went to the door for the umpteenth time. "Husband!" she called. "Bring Grandma Mu's two boxes out from the bottom of the camphor chest next to the back wall."

Soon he passed two packages through the door, one

quite small and one medium sized. They appeared inconsequential with a coarse cotton fabric tightly wrapped around them and tied with a yellowed string.

Slowly, respectfully, Mrs. Mu opened the larger package. As she pushed the final layer of cotton cloth aside, a pair of soft, white, brocade slippers big enough for Mei-hua's feet emerged. Someone had embroidered little flowers around the sides and back. The toes were raised in the auspicious shapes of clouds.

Mei-hua could hardly believe her eyes. These shoes looked like they were made especially for her.

"These were Grandma Mu's wedding shoes. Her family was very poor when she was young; therefore, she, too, never had bound feet. But because of her beauty, a shopkeeper wanted her for a wife. To start her new life off well, her family gave her the best dowry and wedding they could." She gently caressed the flowers along one side, a faraway look in her eyes. She held the shoe out. "Now, you'll wear her shoes. This is an important day for you; it'll change your life, just as her marriage day changed Grandma Mu's life. Therefore, it is right for to you wear these today." With that, Mrs. Mu bent down and slipped the brocade shoes onto her feet. "You will meet the magistrate fully, and appropriately, dressed."

Happy and proud, Mei-hua stood up. "Should I present myself before Master Mu?"

Mrs. Mu smiled. "Not yet, child. There's still one thing missing."

Reaching for the second, smaller package, Mrs. Mu untied the cotton cloth and exposed a lettuce-green jade hairpin carved into the shape of a butterfly. Two strings of variegated green jade beads hung from the head of the hairpin.

"Such a hairpiece could buy a farm, Mistress," Mei-hua exclaimed.

"Yes," Mrs. Mu smiled as she put it into Mei-hua's hair, "but who'd sell it, even to buy a farm?" she asked. "You must wear this, too. It completes the perfect picture."

"Now, we must go present you to Mr. Mu," the older woman said, a satisfied smile lighting her care-worn face. With that she opened the door, and Mei-hua stepped out with a sliding movement, allowing her dress to flow rhythmically about her.

Mr. Mu sat on a three-legged stool, carving an intricate corner piece for a customer. He stopped and put his work aside as Mei-hua entered the room.

As she came to where he was sitting, Mei-hua kneeled and touched her head to the floor, as she would have to her own father on a formal occasion.

"Please, Little One, get up, you don't need to kowtow to us," Mr. Mu admonished.

Without rising, Mei-hua returned, "Master Mu, you and the Mistress have treated me like one of the family. It is only right for me to show my respect."

"Well, then," Mr. Mu said. "if I'm to be as a father to you, stand and let me see what you look like. I can't let my 'daughter' go to the magistrate dressed like a beggar. Or a boy."

Mei-hua glanced up quickly and almost detected a slight grin on his serious face. She dropped her gaze, rose, and stood before him. She tried to look demure, as a girl should, but instead of feeling modest, she felt pleased. Pleased with their gift and how she looked. She was ready to present as strong a case as possible before the magistrate.

Mr. Mu laughed. "Wife! What've you done to the

obedient, clumsy helper we had?" he teased. "Where did this young woman come from?"

There followed a small party of meat-filled pastries and tea, along with some discussion concerning who should accompany Mei-hua and what she should say to the magistrate. In the end, they decided both the carpenter and his wife would go to the court with Mei-hua and, although it may be unusual, Madam Mu should be the one to escort her inside and remain with her through whatever happened.

Mr. Mu ordered a couple of palanquins and the three of them set off.

CHAPTER 21

TWO GUARDS, one on either side of Mei-hua and Madam Mu, ushered them into the courtroom. Scribes, wearing dark robes and small black hats, bent over a long side table busily preparing their ink, ready to record evidence presented to the court. Guards stood in parallel lines forming a straight path to the far end of the hall and a raised platform. The path ended at a massive table covered by a cloth with double dragons stitched across its front. An ornately carved chair in black wood loomed behind the desk. Here, the magistrate sat erect and imposing, as if the sun itself, giving meaning and life to the proceedings.

Mei-hua's legs refused to carry her any further into the room. She couldn't take her eyes off him. He wore the judicial red robe with the *xiè zhì*, a mythical animal representing justice, emblazoned on its chest, and a hard, molded, black gauze cap, which sat squarely on his head. The sight of him had the effect his clothing was designed to have: she was overwhelmed with awe, impressed by the majesty of his office and at the lowliness of her own position. She lost heart; she'd never be able to present her case before this imposing judge. He no longer appeared to be the same Master Hsu she was accustomed to seeing at the house.

Mei-hua stood before him locked in a fog, unable to move or to think coherently for what seemed like hours. A powerful, full voice called out Madam Mu's name. With a start, she looked around and realized she had been standing there for only a few short seconds. Reality came flooding back. She cast a quick glance at Madam Mu whose face showed she had also temporarily lost her bravado.

"Come forward!" Magistrate Hsu called out to the two.

Moving gracefully with short, sliding steps, Mei-hua came forward, Madam Mu at her side. When they reached the place designated for defendants, they both fell to the ground kowtowing, as was the custom for those entering the court.

When they finished kowtowing, neither dared rise; they remained on the floor, two prostrate figures spread before the Judge.

"Stand and approach the court!" he called out in a stern voice.

Mei-hua and Madam Mu rose in unison and stood directly in front of him. They remained silent. No one ever spoke in court unless the judge asked them a question.

"This court is adjourned until the hour of the rooster this evening," Magistrate Hsu announced loudly. In a more moderate voice he added, "Madam Mu and Zhang

Mei-hua, you will come with me."

After giving orders to his assistants, he rose and strode toward the court's back door. Mei-hua and Madam Mu followed as directed, but Mei-hua was confused. Nothing in the magistrate's appearance told her what to expect next. Nothing in his face or eyes indicated he even recognized her. And yet, he must have. Why else was he taking them with him to...where? Were they to be interrogated, taken to jail? Her eyes slid sideways to the white-haired woman beside her. Would the magistrate hold the Mus responsible for what she'd done? She chastised herself once more for getting Madam Mu and the carpenter involved. She hadn't meant to jeopardize the lives of innocent people.

She didn't have long to wait before discovering their destination. As they passed through the curtained door, she recognized Master Hsu's informal working area. Another ornately carved, generous sized desk faced into the room, and a table and chairs for guests filled the opposite corner.

"Please, sit and have some tea," Master Hsu said to Mrs. Mu as he removed his cap and placed it on the table. "Bring tea," he told an assistant standing at attention nearby.

When he left, Master Hsu said, "So, today you are Zhang Mei-hua." He closely examined Mei-hua in her finery. "Certainly you are dressed in a manner becoming the daughter of a notable family. But," he paused, then continued as his iron gaze fell on Mrs. Mu, "now you must tell me what has happened. Isn't that why you escorted the young lady, Madam? To tell this child's story?"

Madam Mu started to rise in order to kowtow again, but he waved her back into her seat with an impatient hand and ordered her to tell him everything she knew. And to leave nothing out.

"Honorable Magistrate Hsu, Little Big ... I mean, Zhang Mei-hua, has been wronged. She is not a criminal. She has been living in our shop, working as our assistant, and I can vouch for her honesty and integrity."

Mei-hua was touched at Madam Mu's speech. By now, however, she had regained her desire to tell her own story, as only she could. With tiny tugs on the elder woman's sleeve, she sought her attention. Unfortunately, such a small gesture couldn't derail Madam Mu who, completely wrapped up in her testimonial for Mei-hua, plunged ahead with her tale. Magistrate Hsu, however, noticed Mei-hua's feeble attempts and a small smile played at the corners of his lips.

Nevertheless, he allowed Madam Mu to say her piece, which contained a lot of good will for the girl and few relevant facts of the case. After she finished, Magistrate Hsu thanked her and directed his assistant, who had returned, to offer her tea and a plate of dried fruits.

"And now, Zhang Mei-hua, what have you to say? Please give us the story behind your many personae," Master Hsu said, his eyes bright with interest.

Mei-hua hoped she caught a softening in his tone, but she wasn't sure. He had every right to be furious with her; she had deceived him and his family. Even though her intentions were honorable, she recognized he may no longer believe her because of her past lies.

Breathing deeply, she dropped her gaze and bowed her head. She began her story. She started with the most critical information: the false charges brought against her father by unscrupulous officials. She told of her journey to Hangzhou with three faithful servants; of being kidnapped by bandits. She spoke of her decision at that time to continue pretending to be mute because her accent would give her away as a young woman from an upper class family and the bandits would have tried to ransom her. If they did, her father's plans to get her, the last of his family, to a safe place would be ruined. She told of being taken to the bandit leader's home and being sold as an indentured servant into the Hsu household. She ended by telling him that on the night of his daughter's attempted kidnapping, Mei-hua, afraid she had been exposed, believed she would now be turned over to her father's enemies. Therefore, she fled, pretending to be a boy, and found work and a place to stay as an apprentice with Master and Madam Mu. She made it clear that the couple had no idea of her real identity, only that she needed a job.

Madam Mu broke in at this point, enthusiastically describing her young charge's conflict with the street thug. Mei-hua explained how the criminal recognized she was the girl abducted by the bandit leader.

During this long and convoluted narrative, Magistrate Hsu said nothing. Now and then he raised his hand, indicating to his servant to refill Madam Mu's tea or bring more fruit and pastries. His face remained impassive. Although his eyes flashed with interest, they did not betray his thoughts or response to their tale.

"And that brought us here, to your court, Your Excellency," Mei-hua finally said, completing her story.

The following few seconds of silence seemed endless. Had she misjudged Master Hsu? Still uncertain about the wisdom of coming to him in court, she wondered if she might have been better off as a fugitive.

Even with no family and no friends to help her.

"You say you are Magistrate Zhang's daughter," he began, breaking the aching silence. "But, I must ask you: what's your proof? Your word alone is not enough in a court."

"Sir, before I left my father's house with my three servants he gave me an amulet to wear. If I can find his friend here in Hangzhou, he would identify it as belonging to my father." She shook her head and frowned. "Unfortunately, he didn't tell me his friend's name. Old Lin handled everything, but now he and the others are gone." Tears welled up in her eyes and slid down her cheeks.

The magistrate waited for a moment, letting her regain her composure. "Of what importance is this amulet? How is it different from the tens of thousands in the market or worn by other people?" His questions were direct but not unkind.

"Sir, my father told me that when he was a student he and several of his *tóng-xué*, his fellow students, formed an alliance in which they promised to always come to each other's aid. They had jade amulets made as a symbol of this friendship. The amulets were all cut from the same stone, the color of brown autumn tea, and inscribed with the words 'When the wind blows, the grass must bend.'"

Mei-hua reached for her neck and fumbled inside her jacket before pulling out a simple silk cord revealing a long, narrow piece of jade. Lifting it over her head, she took the stone in her two hands and offered it to him. "This is my father's amulet, Sir."

Magistrate Hsu took the jade piece and examined it with a grave expression. Without a word, he placed the tea colored jade on the table between them. Leaning back, he removed a long silk cord hidden under his robes. Another jade piece swung from the cord. He placed it next to Mei-hua's father's amulet: they were a perfect pair.

CHAPTER 22

MEI-HUA GASPED. Her heart pounded hard and loud, its drumming seeming to drown out the other sounds in the room. She could not believe her eyes. Could this man, the man who owned her and for whom she was a servant—the man she ran away from—be her father's long sought friend?

Looking up from the twin jade pieces, Magistrate Hsu said, "My dear, you've found your father's *tóng-xué*. I'm sorry you suffered so much in your long search, but at last it is finished." Although it held a hint of sorrow, he allowed a slight smile to cross his lips.

Your father. At the mention of her father, Mei-hua's drumming heart stopped and her face turned paper white.

Magistrate Hsu bent forward and continued in a low, sympathetic voice. "Don't worry, Mei-hua, your father sent me a message saying he's safe, at least for the present. He'd learned of your kidnapping and immediately dispatched his men to find the bandits, but to no avail. Further, besides being his friend and expecting you to come under my protection, I am also the magistrate in the district the abduction took place. Therefore, he sent a messenger informing me of the crime, apprising me of his progress and asking for my assistance. Naturally, I immediately assigned a contingent of solders to scour the countryside looking for clues and the bandits. Also to no avail! Little did we know you had already come under my roof, living as a servant." He shook his head and tapped his right cheek.

Then, flicking a hand toward a servant, he ordered, "Have Guei-lung come in at once."

Turning back to her, he continued. "Mei-hua, you'll continue to remain in my house, although no longer as a bondmaid," at these words, a slight grin to crease his face, "but as my dearest niece. Because your father is my *tóng-xué*, I consider him to be as my brother. Therefore, you, too, are a part of my family and will now join us as my *zhí-nǔ*."

At these words, at his calling her his niece and a member of his family, a flood of emotions swirled around her. She had not only found safety, she once again was part of a family. A sense of warmth and calm she had not experienced since leaving her father's house washed over her.

Turning toward the carpenter's wife, who sat in stunned silence, the magistrate continued, "Madam, your kindness has brought all this about. Without you and your husband Mei-hua would be lost to us. I would like to reward your compassion and generosity."

In spite of the woman's protests, the magistrate directed his servants to fetch a list of items. When they returned, he told them to put the two bolts of fine silk cloth along with many delicacies to eat on the black lacquered table in front of her chair. He took three gold pieces and a handful of silver out of his sleeve and tucked them gently into her hands. Madam Mu stammered at the show of generosity and again tried to rise in order to kowtow. He waved her back into her chair.

"These things are nothing. Please, accept these few worthless gifts as a sign of our appreciation for all you have done for our family," he said. He turned to a servant and instructed him to gather up the gifts and help Madam Mu carry them. "Mei-hua, you stay."

As the dazed woman started to rise, Mei-hua touched her arm: "You and Master Mu saved me. Without you I would be on the streets, alone with no family, no friends. Please don't forget me. I would be honored if you'd come to visit me often. You and Master Mu have been like parents to me. I'll never forget your kindness."

The older woman let the armful of gifts Master Hsu gave her slip to the ground. Embracing Mei-hua she expressed her fondness and care with a classic parental comment: "Make your Father proud and be a good daughter. While you are living here with your Uncle's family you must not be too troublesome and never cause them any worry."

Mei-hua understood the emotion behind these admonitions. She nodded yes to everything the older woman said. She had grown close to Madam Mu and her husband, and leaving was hard. Both Mei-hua's and the kindly older woman's eyes shimmered with tears.

Before the servant escorted Madam Mu out of the inner office, the magistrate repeated Mei-hua's requests for her and her husband to come often to his house and visit his niece.

No sooner had the older woman left, then Guei-lung strode into the room. He cast a questioning glance at Mei-hua and then at his father. Clearly, he wondered what had happened. He waited for Master Hsu to speak.

"Guei-lung, I want you to meet someone. Mei-hua, come here."

Feeling the heat spread through her body and her face, Mei-hua rose from her place and walked to Master Hsu's side.

"Guei-lung, this is your *táng-mèi*, your younger cousin."

Guei-lung possessed a great deal of composure, but he couldn't hide his astonishment at this turn of events. Not only was his father calling the servant girl, Mei-hua, his *táng-mèi*, but the young woman glowed with an even greater elegance and beauty than when they'd been at Aunt Xi's. Words melted away and he remained speechless.

The heat rising in Mei-hua's face grew intense and her ears tingled. She again dropped her eyes.

"Well, son, I see you are as astonished by all this as I was. But here," his father leaned over to pick up the identical jade amulets, "is proof of our ties. Her father is my *tóng-xué* and my sworn brother.

Just as Guei-lung opened his mouth to barrage him with questions, his father held up a hand, stopping him. "You are curious about what happened, of course. In a moment Mei-hua can go with you and explain the long, complicated story." Turning to her, he added, "Your father would be proud of your spirit, ingenuity, and intelligence. You are much like him." He smiled broadly, "Only his child would think of hiding out as a boy in a carpenter's shop!"

At this remark, Guei-lung stared first at his father and then at Mei-hua, who stood before him in complete feminine splendor. His mouth moved, but no words came out.

Fortunately, this was no problem, since his father gave him no time to speak. Master Hsu said, "Mei-hua, I'm sure you've been worried about your father throughout this long period of absence from home. As I said before, he's safe. For now. He has many friends who are working to resolve this terrible situation. We managed to postpone anyone from submitting a formal, although trumped-up, charge against him. Such an action would require an immediate investigation and, in spite of his position in the government, quite possibly his arrest."

Mei-hua's face lost all color, her momentary gaiety wiped away by the thought of her father being hounded by an unknown enemy who could destroy him and everyone he loves.

The magistrate leaned toward her, concern written in his dark eyes. "Take heart. As I say, he has many friends and the elusive monster behind his troubles will be defanged. Nevertheless, yes, he's still in danger. Therefore, you must remain with us, where I can protect you. I'll send him a message right away to let him know you are safe."

He took up her father's golden brown amulet and placed it in her hands before slipping on his own amulet and dropping it under his robes. Mei-hua looked down at her cool, luminous amulet, and thought how it'd helped her in her struggle to find her father's friend; that her father, though still in trouble, was temporarily safe; and that she was once again among family.

"Now, I'm sorry to say it's time for me to get back to court business," Master Hsu said. With a curt nod of his head toward Mei-hua and his son, he continued, "Go into the house, you two. Mei-hua, tell the family your wonderful story. After I finish today's court business, I'll join all of you to celebrate our reunion at dinner."

With the amulet still clutched in her hand, Mei-hua bowed low before him and followed Guei-lung out of the room. They walked through the office door and into a back courtyard. Away from his father's presence, Guei-lung dropped back to walk in step with her. He let his arm press against hers as they moved down the narrow walk encircling the courtyard. As they moved out of hearing range of his father's door, Guei-lung put his hand on her arm and stopped her. His touch set off a riot of pins and needles from her arm through her body. She started, and almost knocked into the wall along the walk.

He pretended not to notice. Standing over her, he bent his head and said, "Mei-hua, you're a true mystery, big feet and all."

They both laughed.

"I hope that as 'cousins' we will enjoy many long hours together, although I wish you were my *biǎo-mèi* rather than my *táng-mèi*."

Mei-hua felt the heat rise in her face again. She hoped he couldn't see her blush at his remark. If she were his *biǎo-mèi*, a cousin from his mother's side of the family, instead of his *táng-mèi*, she would be considered an ideal choice for a wife. As a *táng-mèi*, they were too closely related to be married. She turned her face away.

As they resumed their stroll back to the woman's quarters, she clutched the amulet in her hand. Its coolness reaffirmed her sense of safety. At the same time, she couldn't help but wonder what this new chapter in her life would bring.

THE END

Author's Note: Mei-hua's World

THE EVENTS IN *HIDDEN* take place in 1380, during the politically tumultuous era just after the fall of the Yuan Dynasty (1271–1368) and at the beginning of the Ming Dynasty (1368–1644). While I have attempted to be as true to the period as possible, all of the characters are fictional. Their lives reflect what could have happened given the culture and society of the time.

Similar to contemporary China, most people who lived under both the Yuan and Ming Dynasties identified as being ethnically Han. However, for the nearly 100 years of the Yuan Dynasty, China was ruled by Mongolians, a neighboring but non-native ethnic group. As non-Han, they spoke a different language and did not use Chinese characters in their writing. Throughout the Yuan Dynasty official documents were in both Mongolian and Chinese.

Although there was a small contingent of Mongolian officials in the highest ranks of government, most of the people who ran the country—including the magistrates—were highly educated Han Chinese like Mei-hua's father. While the rulers relied on the competence of their native officials, they did not want them to become too powerful. Therefore, the Han officials were not allowed to learn Mongolian, and spoke and wrote only in Chinese dialects. As a result, interpreters were needed to intervene between the rulers, their government workers, and the people of China. This role was aptly played by other non-Han ethnic groups from the north and west, such as the Uyghur people (Mei-hua's mother's ethnic group).

Between the end of the Yuan and the beginning of the Ming Dynasties, there were many years of warfare, unrest, and banditry. Hong-wu (who ruled from 1368 to 1398), established the Ming Dynasty, which represented a return to power by the Han Chinese. Although he eventually brought law and order throughout the country, it was not easy to establish control after years of warfare. As the first Emperor of the dynasty, Hong-wu kept a constant vigil looking for usurpers who wanted to destroy him and establish their own dynasty. Hong-wu was brutal and unflinching in his rooting out of even a hint of traitorous behavior. He not only obliterated anyone he believed to be against him, but he also destroyed several generations of their families as a means of ripping out the problem by its roots.

1380 was a particularly bad period for Hong-wu's would-be enemies. In that year alone, he killed thousands of people, including many of his officials and their families. Not only spouses and children, but also grandparents, parents, brothers, sisters, in-laws, uncles, aunts, cousins, grandchildren, and even grandnephews and –nieces of convicted traitors could be executed. It was one of several times Hong-wu purged his government, and was the perfect opportunity for high-placed officials to get rid of their rivals by implicating them in treasonous behavior. It is this unsettled world that Mei-hua and her father find themselves.

Chinese Names

Given Names

In China, given names indicate the expectations as well as the importance of a person, often reflecting the parents' hopes and dreams for their child. Therefore, parents try to pick names that either represent good fortune or reflect the type of personality they hope their child will have. For example, "Ping-an" means "quiet and peaceful." Her name reflects her parents' highest aspiration for her: to marry and be a good wife and daughter-in-law. They wanted her to have an easy disposition which would allow her to fit into her husband's family without creating problems. Guei-lung's name, however, means "precious dragon." "Precious" indicates he is important to them as a son, while "dragon" refers to their expectations that he will be successful in his career and life.

Mei-hua is the word for plum blossom, a hardy flower which blooms in the winter and is the first sign of spring. Therefore, the Mei-hua flower is a symbol of perseverance, strength, hope, purity, and beauty—all characteristics Magistrate Zhang wanted his daughter to have. When she becomes a bond servant, she is also coincidentally called Mei-hua, but for other reasons. Flower names were common for girls, and Ping-an rather thoughtlessly assigned the new bondservant the moniker based on a piece of jewelry she happened to receive that day. The young mistress's carelessness reflects how unimportant people thought servants' names were.

Family Names

Chinese society is patrilineal, meaning people trace their ancestry through their father's side and children usually take their father's last name. Also, unlike English names, in Chinese the family name always comes first, followed by the person's given name. Mei-hua's full name is Zhang Mei-hua; her father's name is Zhang Xue-Wen. Ping-an's father is Hsu Dou-wu and her name is Hsu Ping-an.

For married women, the use of a family name was more complex. In the United States and many Western countries, women often drop their own family name when they marry and take their husband's family name. This was not the case in traditional China. While women may be referred to by their husband's name, as we see with Mrs. Mu, they also keep their own family names. This is because they belong to a different family lineage than their husband. An upper class woman, such as Aunt Xi, would be referred to by her own family name and not her husband's. On the other hand, while village women and commoners would also keep their own family names, they were often addressed by their relationship to others. For example, Mrs. Mu is Mr. Mu's wife. If they had children, she could also be addressed as the mother of that child.

Within the family, people are often called by their relationship to the speaker. Ping-an, for example, would normally call her brother *Gē-ge* (older brother) rather than by his given name, Guei-lung. He would call her *Mèi-mei* (younger sister) and not Ping-an. However, because this could become confusing for the English reader, I chose to have each person refer to the other by their given name.

Where people lived

In *Hidden* there are three different types of houses. Two of these belong to the average citizen: the simple rectangular home and the U-shaped house centered around a courtyard. The third home in the story is the personal residence of the magistrate, which is a part of a large complex of buildings that also included the local government's offices and the court. This cluster of official and personal spaces occupied by a magistrate is called a *yamen*.

The working poor and modest farmers—that is, the majority of people—lived in the simplest houses: a one room rectangle with a single door in the center of the front wall. The only windows were in the front, usually with one set on either side of the door. The family cooked, slept, and lived in this single room. A stove made out of bricks and mud was built into one corner for preparing their meals. Often a *kang*, a raised sleeping platform made out of bricks, would take up half or more of the room's space. This is where the family sat during the day and slept at night. In *Hidden*, Mother Yang and Ben-ji's small home did not even have a kang for sleeping.

Wealthier households, such as that of Ping-an and Guei-lung's aunt and uncle, had multiple rooms in their homes. Such houses were added to over time as the family's fortune increased, typically forming a U-shaped structure out of a set of connected rooms flowing around a central courtyard. The courtyard made up as much as 40% of the entire residential area. These were spacious, generous sized homes that faced inward. An interior veranda allowed the family to move comfortably from one part of their home to another. Large walls surrounded the home to ensure privacy, and a gate opened to the street. In these complexes, the center building faced south and was where the senior members of the family, such as parents and grandparents, lived. Married sons and their families lived in the buildings running down the east and west sides of the complex. This pattern expanded and became more elaborate as the family's wealth increased. This is the case with Ping-an and Guei-lung's uncle's home, which consists of multiple buildings and interior courtyards. If you were to visit it, you would come into an outer courtyard that served as a place for receiving visitors, especially male visitors. Next, you would go through a wide building and enter the inner courtyard, where the members of the house carry out their everyday activities, such as recreation, study, and household record keeping. After going through another wide building you would reach what is called the "inner apartments" or "women's area," where Ping-an and her mother's rooms are. Servants lived and slept in yet another area, which could be located wherever it was convenient for the family, usually near the front or side of the house complex. This is where Mei-hua and the other maids share a room. Within the courtyards and in other open spaces, such as between the family's buildings and the outside walls, there would be gardens for beauty and general enjoyment as well as gardens for growing vegetables and herbs. A garden and minor, unimportant buildings and sheds would be found along the compound's high exterior wall.

Finally, the most complex and elite form of housing was the yamen. These multi-use compounds were where magistrates lived with their families and carried out their duties as government officials. The yamen was located in the center of the city and covered a large area, perhaps even several blocks. The front consisted of public buildings for the government, including the court. The middle section held offices for the magistrate and his staff, as well as an area for receiving official visitors. Finally, the magistrate and his family lived in a generous area at the back of the complex. The magistrate lived in the government's compound because he only held office in any given province for a maximum of three years; then he was transferred to his next post as magistrate in another province. This system was followed in order to avoid corruption. At the same time, as the highest ranking person in the city, magistrates needed housing suitable to their positions. Thus, the yamen was both the magistrate's office and home.

Separation of the sexes

A strict separation of the sexes was considered important, not only in public, but also in the house. In wealthy families, all children lived and played in the inner parts of the house where their mothers lived. However, as the children grew up, the girls stayed with their mothers in the inner, women's quarters and the boys moved into the outer rooms. This physical separation also reflected the way society saw men's and women's roles. The women were responsible for the household (represented by the inner courtyard and buildings), and the men were in charge of everything outside the house (represented by the middle courtyard and buildings). It was considered bad manners for the men of the house to spend time in the women's quarters during the day. Even male servants were not to go into the women's area unless they were making repairs or assisting in some important task. At the same time, women were not allowed out of the inner quarters without good reason.

Obviously, this kind of separation between men and women within the family requires a large house.

Therefore, only the very wealthy could afford to live this way. Among the poor and middle classes, all members of the family lived in close proximity to each other. Given that the kang was the only space for sleeping in a modest home, the entire family must of necessity have slept together on it. Quite a different lifestyle from the elite class.

Medicine, Religion, and Science

In the story, Ping-an's near suicide is dealt with through both spiritual and medical treatment. Traditionally, Chinese medical practice involved a close relationship between religion and science, which were not separated in the way they often are today. In Ming China, the supernatural elements of life—what we now associate with religion—were simply understood as an extension of the everyday world. As a result, when a person was sick they could be tended to by a Buddhist monk, a Daoist priest, a medically trained doctor from the national medical school, or an itinerant doctor (often called a bell doctor). Bell doctors learned the art of healing through an apprenticeship. Their training varied considerably and depended largely on the skill and knowledge of their particular teacher. The Daoist priest could be a medium, a kind of conduit between the spiritual world and the material world. During a ceremony the medium would invite the spirit to possess his body. While possessed, the medium would be able to determine what caused the illness or problem: bad fate or karma, a psychic debt, or some other problem in the nether world. With this knowledge the medium could cure his client, usually through a combination of medicines and spiritual treatments.

It was common for people to use one or all of these

specialists because each brought a different ability to help cure the client and keep her from becoming ill again. For example, a Daoist priest would probably give his client a talisman to protect her from illnesses and a Buddhist monk would say prayers.

Final Comments

Mei-hua's world represents a continuation of tradition in the midst of social upheaval. Despite the political shifts between the Yuan and Ming periods, certain strong themes remained consistent, including the importance of family, a hierarchical social structure, and the presence of the supernatural in everyday life. It is in this world that we find Mei-hua trying to survive.

Made in the USA
San Bernardino, CA
27 December 2016